THE
WILD ONES

GREAT ESCAPE

THE
WILD ONES

GREAT ESCAPE

C. Alexander London

PHILOMEL BOOKS

PHILOMEL BOOKS

an imprint of Penguin Random House LLC
375 Hudson Street, New York, NY 10014

Text copyright © 2017 by C. Alexander London.
Map of Ankle Snap Alley copyright © 2015 by Levi Pinfold.
Interior art and map of zoo copyright © 2017 by Levi Pinfold.

Library of Congress Cataloging-in-Publication Data is available upon request.

Printed in the United States of America.
ISBN 9780399171017
1 3 5 7 9 10 8 6 4 2

Edited by Jill Santopolo.   Design by Semadar Megged.
Text set in 12.25-point Winchester New ITC Std.

To Tim, who's sharing this wild adventure with me

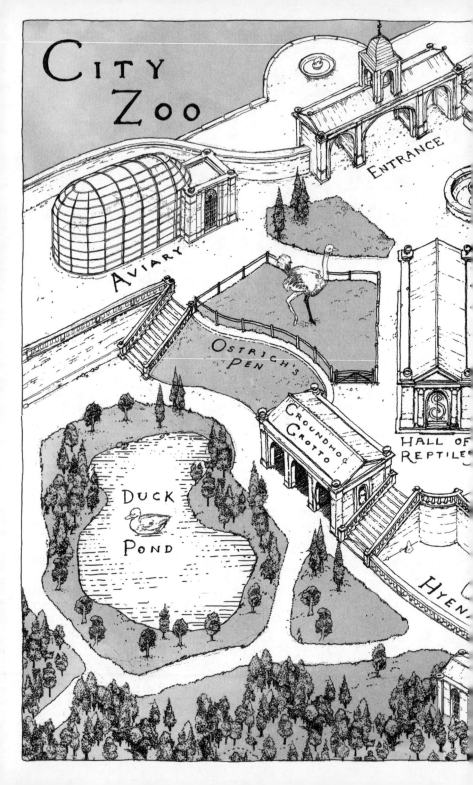

A SQUIRREL IN SPRING

A squirrel makes a plan. That is how a squirrel survives.

Balanced high on a wire or leaping from branch to branch, even while quietly nibbling on a pilfered peanut, a squirrel is always planning his next move.

After the wire, I'll leap to the tree, a wise squirrel thinks. *And after the tree, I'll jump to the garden. If there's a dog in the garden, I'll go under the fence. If I lose one acorn in the tree stump, I'll hide five more behind the shed.*

Climb or jump, dig or sit, scurry, bury, or just plain

run: *A squirrel who doesn't think ahead is a squirrel who surely winds up dead.*

That was the saying anyway, but Dax, who considered himself a Squirrel of Action, didn't like to waste time with planning and worrying and thinking things through. Leap first and let his tail to do the thinking in the air, that was Dax's way.

And so he ran across the wire without a plan in his nut-sized brain. He did, however, have a bucktoothed grin splitting his face. He loved to climb up to the highest point he could reach over Ankle Snap Alley, just so he could feel the cool dawn breeze blowing across his fur with the first whiff of spring on its breath. Sunrise was his favorite time, when the sky painted itself pink and the nighttime animals all made their scuttling ways to bed.

Possum Ansel closed his bakery, and Enrique Gallo, the retired fighting rooster, locked the door of his barbershop. Moles rushed home beneath the dirt and even the wily Blacktail brothers, gambling raccoons of ill repute, closed their games and pocketed their winnings, shuffling off to trade the seeds and nuts for some piping-hot fishbone broth to put some meat back on their raccoon bones. Winter had ended and spring had sprung at last.

Folks got skinny while they slept through the cold months, but not Dax. He hadn't gotten even the least bit hungry over winter like a lot of other creatures did. His mom was a planner and she had seeds and nuts stored all over Ankle Snap Alley, in more hidey-holes than even she could remember. She didn't use the Reptile Bank and Trust, because she didn't believe in leaving all her seeds in one spot, so she hadn't been that worried when the bandit Coyote and his gang of otters tried to rob it at the start of the season. She knew she'd be all right no matter what.

Other squirrels in Dax's class sometimes found the hidden nuts and took them home to their parents and Dax's mother didn't mind.

"Most folks in Ankle Snap Alley aren't as lucky as we are," his mother told him. "This is a neighborhood with more concrete than grass, and not all animals are so well suited to it. We who have a lot, have a lot to share. What kind of squirrels would we be if we kept all our nuts to ourselves while other folk shivered and starved?"

Dax liked having such a thoughtful mother because it meant he didn't have to think quite so much himself. Someone else worried about keeping his belly full, so he could focus on his adventures.

He did his best to make his mother proud. He was the kind of squirrel who picked the fleas out of someone else's fur before flicking off his own. He'd even joined the Moonlight Brigade, training after school all winter to protect the wild world, and doing spy missions for his classmate Kit, the Moonlight Brigade's young raccoon leader.

Dax was a soldier in the brigade and he liked following a soldier's orders, because it meant he didn't have to make plans of his own. He could have adventures without all the trouble of thinking them up!

This morning his adventure involved running across the wire on official brigade business. He had to tell Kit what he'd learned from a scurry of chipmunks who had just been to a family reunion in another neighborhood. These chipmunks had cousins who'd told them something terrifying, something that Kit and all the creatures of Ankle Snap Alley *needed* to know.

The alley was in danger! It wasn't Flealess house pets or criminal coyotes this time . . . Their enemy was far more dangerous, and far more clever, maybe even cleverer than Kit himself!

Standing high over Ankle Snap Alley, Dax thought about the fastest way to Kit's front door: scurrying down the pole. He also thought about the most exciting way to Kit's front door, which meant making the long leap from the pole to the edge of the fence, running across the wire until he got to the rooftop of Possum Ansel's bakery, flipping to the ground, begging Ansel to give him a delicious gum-and-onion-peel chew pie before closing, and *then* knocking on Kit's door.

Dax chose the pie way.

No matter the danger, a squirrel will always choose the way that leads past pie.

Dax bent his back legs and thrust himself into the air, stretching out his front claws and twirling his bushy tail for balance. His whiskers waved and for a moment he was weightless. Then, he caught the fence and swung himself onto its upper edge, scurried along, and jumped down to Ansel's roof and from there to the ground.

He knocked, but he was too late. Ansel had closed up shop. The sun was up and just about any animal with any sense was climbing into bed. The day belonged to the People and the moonlight folk did their best to stay out of the People's way.

Dax looked down the alley and saw his mother pop her head out from their apartment to look for him. He ducked behind the bakery so she couldn't see him. He didn't want to go home yet. He *had* to tell Kit what he'd learned from the chipmunks.

Once his mother put her head back inside the tree trunk and closed the window, Dax crept out. He stepped carefully, moving in a zigzag toward Kit's front door. The first sprouts of spring weeds smushed under his paws and meltwater mud made a sucking sound when he scampered across it.

His gaze caught on a whole peanut resting in a dandelion

patch. Someone must have dropped it on the way home. One of the birds, maybe, or another squirrel? It wasn't a gum-and-onion-peel chew pie, but it was still something to eat. He thought of his mother and how generous she was. She'd hate to see a peanut wasted. She'd be so proud of him for bringing it home. Maybe they'd even donate it to an orphan mouse. Mice were always losing their parents at winter's end.

He scampered over to the peanut and scooped it up without thinking.

A wise squirrel would have thought before scooping.

In Ankle Snap Alley, a peanut is never just left lying in the weeds for no reason. In Ankle Snap Alley, a peanut in the weeds is hiding something.

Something like a trap.

Just as Dax grabbed the peanut—SNAP!

A plastic box burst from the dirt and snapped shut around him.

"Ahhh! Help!" he yelled, but he was stuck inside the box and his little claws couldn't find an opening. He banged and jostled and scratched and pried, but he was totally trapped inside.

The People had caught him.

With all the wild folk headed to bed for the day, no one was around to help him.

"Helphelphelp!" he yelled, and stomped, crushing the

cursed peanut into paste below his feet. He banged and hollered so much, he wore himself out and got drowsy. His eyes shut while his little fists were still banging, and he fell into a stupor. When he came back to his senses, he felt the trap being lifted from the ground and he knew a Person was taking it away with him inside it.

"But I have to warn Kit . . . ," he muttered. "Kit needs to know . . . I have to warn everyone . . . about the People . . . the People are coming for us all . . ."

But no one could hear him inside the trap and that was how Dax the squirrel disappeared during the early days of spring.

He was the first animal to vanish from Ankle Snap Alley that season, but he was not the last.

Part I

~~~

THE
URBAN WILD

Chapter One

SHADOW TRAPPING

HOW do you catch a shadow?

Kit puzzled over that question from the safety of the Dumpster where he hid, standing on his back paws, his little black eyes peering through the black mask of fur on his face. His whiskers twitched while his front claws tapped a *rat-tat-tat* on the Dumpster's metal edge.

He had perched himself on a mushy black trash bag, which he had, of course, first torn open to inspect the garbage inside. People, he'd noticed, threw away amazing quantities of lettuce and bread crusts and cheese rinds with hardly any mold on any of it.

Now that he'd had a snack, he was ready to capture the shadow.

He squinted against the shimmering sunlight overhead. The shadow was an afternoon hunter, and against all Kit's raccoon instincts, he had to be wide awake in broad daylight to catch it. Other raccoons were sound asleep, along with the sensible bats and possums and rats. But Kit wasn't interested in being any kind of sensible. He was interested in catching his quarry.

Of course, it wasn't the shadow he was after, but the bird of prey making the shadow, a red-tailed hawk named Valker. Kit had some questions he needed answered and only Valker could answer them.

However, no one in Ankle Snap Alley had ever spoken to Valker before, or at least no one who was still around to talk about it. Valker was a merciless hunter with a beak like a razor blade and eyes just as sharp. By the time any of the scurrying residents of Ankle Snap Alley saw more than Valker's shadow, a flash of feather, say, or a grasping talon, it was already too late.

One moment a little mouse could be standing outside the store considering which sort of cheese she'd like to purchase for a Church Mouse Supper, and the next, she'd be snatched into the sky without so much as a squeak.

Animals had been vanishing from Ankle Snap Alley since spring began and if Valker wasn't the one responsible, he'd at least know who was. It was Kit's job, as leader of the Moonlight Brigade and sworn protector of Ankle Snap Alley, to find out what was happening to his neighbors.

The Hawk would have to be persuaded to tell Kit . . . and also not to crush Kit's skull in the process.

Kit had one advantage, though. He had his best friend, Eeni.

Eeni was a white rat who was braver than Valker was fast, and cleverer than Valker was deadly. At least, that's what she'd told Kit when she'd volunteered to help him with his plan to catch the hawk.

"It'll be easy as sneaking the socks off a centipede," she'd said the night before, but now Kit saw her confidence falter as Valker's shadow passed overhead. Kit had long ago noticed how boasts made in moonlight usually dissolved under a midday sun.

Still, frightened though she was, Eeni kept her promise. She was a rat of her word.

She was also the only the creature who hadn't taken cover from Valker, circling above. While other folks were asleep in their burrows and nests, Eeni was out in the wide-open alley, without so much as a leaf over her back, limping as she staggered between the entrance to Possum Ansel's Sweet & Best-Tasting Baking Company and the

Dancing Squirrel Theater across the way. Her tiny pink paws clutched at the ground and her limp-legged stutter-steps dragged her far too slowly to make a getaway.

To a hunter like Valker, "fast food" was the food that ran the slowest. Eeni must have looked like a delightful afternoon snack.

The hawk whirled on the breeze, spreading wide his white-tipped wings, then turned in a slow arc until his shadow was directly over Eeni, shading her beneath his blue-black outline.

"Ohh ohhh no!" she cried, looking up at him. "Oh no! It's Valker! Someone help me!"

She glanced at Kit in his Dumpster. Her little eyes widened as she took a small hop toward him. Her back leg dragged behind her and her limp made her too slow to reach the safety of the Dumpster before Valker attacked.

She took another faltering step, then another, then one more. "Ow!" she grunted with each step. "Ow! Ow!"

She was too slow by half.

"Come on, Eeni . . . ," Kit whispered. "Come on . . ."

A screech from above stopped her where she stood. The shadow dove, fast as lightning, and Eeni curled into herself, clamping her eyes shut, paws over her ears, prayers to the Great Mother Rat on her lips as the winged raptor bore down, talons grasping for Eeni's fragile little bones.

"Ahhh!" she yelled.

"Screech!" Valker screeched.

"Eeni!" Kit cried from the safety of the Dumpster. "Now!"

At Kit's shout, Eeni darted, her limp disappearing, and the hawk's talons caught only her paw prints in the dirt. The hawk had fallen for her trick, just as she'd known he would.

Valker crashed into the ground in a heap of brown and red feathers, then rolled, flapping to a dusty stop. The hawk hopped up onto his legs again, towering as tall as the little shops of the alley. He ruffled and fluffed his feathers, looked around to make sure no one else had seen his embarrassing miss, and then narrowed his pale yellow eyes at Eeni, still all alone out in the open of Ankle Snap Alley.

A breeze blew down the way, rustling a bag that had snagged in a bare branch of the Gnarly Oak Apartments. The wind whistled through the plastic, making it snap and shush.

Kit shivered in the Dumpster. Though the spring air was warm, his blood ran cold. From this close, Valker could probably count the hairs on Kit's best friend's throat.

Eeni gulped.

"Ye think ye can treek me, ratty?" the hawk screeched at her, his birdish accent making all his words sound like ancient curses. He lifted a talon to study where it had whacked into the ground, then swiveled his head to look back at Eeni. "Aye stubbed me toes!"

"Sorry about that." Eeni opened her paws. "I just didn't want to get eaten."

"Yer too late fer that, leetle one. Yer lunch meat now!" Valker charged at her, his beak snapping at her tiny face.

She took a single step backward, away from him, and as he lunged, flapping, he fell flat on his chest, beak-first into the dirt and broken concrete of Ankle Snap Alley. "Ooof!"

Eeni grinned.

Valker had to twist his neck around to see that his ankles were caught. Two moles had popped up from the ground and tied his feet so hopelessly in old dental floss that it might take a team of beavers to chew him free. He flapped ferociously, but the moles heaved him back down. They'd anchored the floss to the base of the Dumpster, and strong as Valker was, he could hardly haul a Dumpster into the sky.

"You're caught, Valker." Eeni grinned at him. "My pals of the paw in the Moonlight Brigade trapped you. You won't be eating the likes of me any time soon."

"Untie meee now!" he yelled. "Or aye'll call down a flock of fury the likes of which ye tiny leetle ones ain't never seen!"

"I wouldn't go around judging folk by their size," Kit said as he heaved himself out of the Dumpster and jumped to the ground. "We may not be big folk here in Ankle Snap, but we've chased off badder beasts than you. Ask what happened to the old coyote who came here looking for trouble."

"You're . . . *Kit?*" Valker let out a hummingbird-sized chirp. He was a hawk who knew most of what went on in the city beneath the Slivered Sky, and he certainly knew about Kit's winning battles against anyone who messed with the good folks of Ankle Snap Alley.

Well, the folks of Ankle Snap Alley weren't exactly "good." Eeni was a notorious pickpocket, the moles dug their way into whatever places they pleased no matter who the places belonged to, and Kit himself could trick a tom-cat out of its tail if he chose to, but even though the alley was filled with gamblers, crooks, liars, and cheats of all kinds, it was home and it looked after its own.

Nobody, no matter how sharp their teeth or strong their talons, could push the folks in Ankle Snap Alley around, not without getting pushed right back twice as hard by Kit and his Moonlight Brigade.

And Valker knew it.

He'd picked the wrong rat to snack on.

Kit shook the dirt from his fur and strolled up beside the hawk, confident as can be. With his talons tangled,

Valker was helpless. He could flap his wings and snap his beak, but all he'd do was wear himself out.

"I just want to ask you a few questions about the folk who've been disappearing," Kit told the hawk. "And then we'll let you go on your way."

After Dax the squirrel disappeared, the Liney sisters—three gray rats who went to school with Kit—had vanished from their home. A few mornings later, a gopher named Sebastian went missing, and then three more squirrels—Dax's mother and two old-timers who didn't run quite so fast as they used to. Every night when the creatures woke up, they'd find another of their neighbors had disappeared.

"Aye dunno nothin' about folk disappearin'," the hawk said, which was the answer Kit had expected. It'd been his experience that the more a creature knew, the less he wanted to talk. Put another way, folk who talked the most usually knew the least.

"So you *do* know something?" Eeni said as she stepped right up to the hawk to tap her little knuckles on his beak like she was knocking on a door. "*I dunno nothin'* is a double negative. You say you don't know nothing, which means you *do* know *something* and the something you know is exactly what we want to know now."

The hawk frowned and twisted his head all the way upside down, which would have been alarming if Kit hadn't done some research beforehand and learned that a confused hawk will often swivel its neck upside down. Eeni's words had befuddled the bird—like they befuddled Kit sometimes too—and a befuddled bird was just what Kit wanted.

"What my friend means to say," Kit said, "is that we know you see everything that goes on in this city from your perch high in the sky, and we only want to know about one thing and as soon as we know it, you'll be untied and terrifying rodents again in no time. I swear from howl to snap. But if you don't answer us . . ." Kit let his voice trail off, then he whistled once.

At his whistle, the door to Possum Ansel's Sweet & Best-Tasting Baking Company opened and out stepped Otis the badger, the biggest, baddest, burliest baking badger anyone had ever seen. He had in his mighty paw a buzzing nest of bees.

"Ansel was gonna use these bees for a spicy pepper-and-honey pie," Otis said. "But they could sting a hawk before we cook 'em, I suppose."

The hawk squeaked again. "Ye wouldn't!"

"He would," said Kit.

"Ye *couldn't*," said the hawk.

"He could," said Kit.

"Ye . . . *shouldn't?*" the hawk tried as Otis stepped closer with the buzzing bees.

"Who says?" Kit replied. "You were gonna eat my friend Eeni, after all. We may look civilized, Valker, but this is the wild world, and we Wild Ones don't do *shoulds*."

Otis stopped and the hawk shivered.

Kit really hoped the bird would give in to his threat, because he was not really going to make the bees sting the bird. Kit knew the reputation he had now that he'd chased off the Flealess house pets and Coyote and his gang from Ankle Snap Alley. Rumors could be just as sharp as claws, and twice as dangerous. He hoped his reputation was dangerous enough that he wouldn't have to do anything to hurt the hawk.

Kit actually *did* live by a code of *shoulds*. He had learned well from his mother, from his uncle Rik, and from his friends: that he *should* be loyal and true, that he *should* be generous and forgiving, and that he *should* always protect the creatures who were less quick of claw than he was. But what was he supposed to do when his *should* for kindness conflicted with his *should* to protect his neighbors? How could he decide which *should* was more important?

Luckily, the hawk couldn't see the conflict in Kit's thoughts and believed Kit's threat completely. When threatened with a nest of buzzing bees, most folks will believe whatever you want them to. Nobody likes to get stung.

"Okee, Kit, aye'll talk," Valker said.

Kit smiled. "Smart choice for a birdbrain. So who is taking our friends?"

"The People!" said Valker. "I see them come in a big rolling box and they snap up your folks in traps, and take 'em away."

"Where?" Eeni insisted. "Where do they take our folks?"

The hawk's eyes darted around. "Don't make me say it," he pleaded. He snapped his beak shut.

"Say it," Eeni ordered him.

"Nuh-uh." Valker shook his head.

"Say it now!" Eeni repeated.

"Nuh-uh." Valker shook his head harder.

Kit frowned and twitched his whiskers. *What* didn't the hawk want to say? What place could be so scary for a hawk that he wouldn't even say the word aloud?

And then Kit knew. It was a word he'd heard just at the start of winter, a word that had rattled in his brain all through the chilly months of waiting for the frost to break. It was a People's word.

His heartbeat quickened as he asked, "Is it *the zoo*?"

At the word *zoo*, Valker the hawk, famed killer from the clouds, squeaked like a mouse and fainted with fright.

"What's so scary about the zoo?" Eeni wondered aloud. "*Zoo* is kind of a dumb word if you ask me. Just saying it sounds silly. Zoo. Zooooo. Zoozoozoo. Scary words should be longer. Like *ravenous* or *decapitated* or *diarrhetic*."

But Kit didn't think the word *zoo* needed to be long to be scary. In the strange and simple sound of those three letters Z-O-O were held all his fears and all his hopes. Just at the start of winter, he'd been told that *the zoo* was where he would find the animal he most wanted to see in the whole world, the animal who had been gone since the leaves first changed in autumn, and whom Kit had long believed he'd never see again. Whom he had thought was dead.

His mother.

She wasn't dead.

She was in a zoo.

And so were all the missing animal folk of Ankle Snap Alley.

Chapter Two

CATCH AND RELEASE

"YOU should be turned into a hat if you let him go!" Blue Neck Ned shouted into Kit's face.

The pigeon's breath smelled like garlic bread crumbs and the blue-and-white feathers around his neck puffed and heaved. His little eyes bulged behind his beak and his shouting turned into a nonsensical series of squawks and grunts.

Kit could have plugged his ears and still seen how mad the pigeon was, because a few of the angry bird's feathers fell out with every furious flap of his wings.

The rest of the crowd squeezed into every nook and cranny of the dimly lit saloon, agreeing with their own calls and quacks and screeches and howls. The neighbors were arguing about what should be done with Valker the Hawk.

The other birds and all the mice agreed with Ned especially loudly.

"He can't be released!" they shouted. "Never!"

It was a rare time indeed when the white-robed church mice agreed with a no-good pigeon like Blue Neck Ned. It seemed like all the folk of fur and feather from one end of Ankle Snap Alley to the other had gathered inside Larkanon's Public House to shout at Kit, although Brevort the skunk had been there before the community meeting and would probably be there long after. He came for the cheese ale. Everyone else had come to yell at Kit.

The hawk himself was tied up with plastic bags and bound tight along the whole length of the saloon's counter.

"He told us what we wanted," Kit said. "I promised I'd let him go if he told us what we wanted. Fair's fair."

"Mmm mmm," Valker agreed, nodding eagerly. He couldn't say anything else because they'd hooded his head with plastic bags too, and tied his beak shut, leaving only a space for his nostrils to breathe through.

"He told *you* what *you* wanted," Shane Blacktail snarled. He was a raccoon like Kit, but he liked Kit about as much as a tick likes turpentine.

"We didn't hear nothing of no use to us," Shane's twin brother, Flynn Blacktail, replied.

"Well, that's another double negative," Eeni piped up on Kit's side, but Shane and Flynn bared their teeth and she let the grammar lesson drop. Sometimes being right wasn't worth being chewed up and spat out. Sometimes it was, but correcting someone else's grammar was almost never one of those times.

"This was a mission of the Moonlight Brigade," said Mr. Timinson, the well-dressed fox who was Kit's teacher and top advisor to the young members of the Moonlight Brigade. "As leader of the Moonlight Brigade, it is surely Kit's decision whether or not he will let his prisoner go free."

"Who put a little raccoon like him in charge anyway?" Blue Neck Ned objected.

"You did," said Mr. Timinson, as calmly as he could. "All of you put him in charge when you let Kit defend you time and time again. He has earned his leadership by acting as a leader, by saving your homes while you all hid in your burrows or fought among yourselves. That is why he gets to decide what to do with his own prisoner. He caught the hawk, so he gets to decide the hawk's fate."

"Well, what if the Rabid Rascals wanted a word with that hawk, eh? What if we *take* the hawk right back from Kit?" Shane asked, raising his claws.

"The Rabid Rascals would have to go through the Moonlight Brigade first!" Eeni replied, showing her own tiny claws to the raccoon. Behind her, Fergus the frog, the two mole twins, Guster and Guster Two (mole parents were not very good at thinking of names), and a tough rabbit named Hazel all held up their claws. Even Mr. Timinson growled in Kit's defense.

Flynn put a paw on his brother's shoulder and the raccoon lowered his claws.

"We don't need to fight each other," Kit said. He didn't have much patience for the Rabid Rascals. They were gangsters who stole from helpless rabbits and voles, but hid in their holes when it was time for real dangerous work to be done. The only reason Kit hadn't had his young Moonlight Brigade wipe out the Rabid Rascals gang altogether was because they were a tradition of Ankle Snap Alley and traditions were not shed as easily as snakeskins.

They were still around, the Old Boss Turtle in his broken van, and the Blacktail brothers with their gambling games, but nobody paid the Rascals much attention anymore, and nobody paid them any of their seeds and nuts anymore either, not since Kit had said they didn't have to. They could still gamble and scowl and cheat and lie—those were Ankle Snap Alley traditions too—but they couldn't go robbing folks anymore. Shane and Flynn were still pretty upset about that.

Now, in spite of his having saved his neighbors from the gangsters, and from the Flealess house pets, and from a vicious coyote and his gang too, all Kit's neighbors were turning on him for wanting to show mercy to a hawk who had told them what they wanted to know.

"You must understand," said Martyn the church mouse, clasping his little claws in front of his crisp white robe, "Valker has eaten more of my cousins than I've ever met. We mice should like to discuss the matter with him ourselves."

A few of the church mice behind Martyn cracked their little mouse knuckles and Valker shuddered. In spite of Martyn's kindly tone and scholarly bearing, it was widely known that most church mice were warriors and sometimes they used the word *discuss* when they meant the word *punch*.

"He's my prisoner and I told him I would let him go," said Kit. "I gave him my word, from howl to snap. So that's what I'm going to do. He gave me valuable information that all of you should care about. He told me where they've been taking our folk. He told me about the People's *zoo.*"

"What do we care about their zoo?" a slick frog in a shiny jacket sneered. "The People mind their business and we mind ours. That's how it is and that's how it should be."

"Except they *aren't* minding their business," Eeni objected.

"They're kidnapping our friends," Kit finished her thought, the way friends sometimes do. "And I think they've got my mother there too!"

"So now the truth comes out," said Shane.

"Young Kit don't care a whisker about our folk," said Flynn. "He just want his mommy back."

Kit reached into his seed-and-nut pouch and touched the small wooden token he kept there. The token was inscribed with the symbol of the Moonlight Brigade, a tiny mouse paw within a rat paw, within a raccoon's paw, within a dog's, on and on up to a bear's massive hand. The paws-within-paws token had been Kit's mother's and when he'd first learned she still lived, he had sworn he would return it to her. He had promised himself, her memory, and the moon above that he would find her again and they would be reunited.

"So what if I do want my mother back?" Kit snarled at Shane and Flynn Blacktail. "I saved your hides more times than a centipede can count on his toes and now you're yelling at me for trying to save my own family?"

Shane shrugged. Flynn frowned.

"She is my family too." An old raccoon sighed from his seat. Kit's uncle Rik stood and padded his way up to his nephew. He gave Kit a pitying look and placed a paw on his shoulder. "I want to find your mother as well," he said. "But you should know that Valker had a bee's nest buzzing in his face and would've said anything to get you to let him go. Wild folks don't take kindly to being held captive and you can't trust a word that hawk tells you. He would say the sky is lettuce and the moon a chunk of cheese if it would set him free. Perhaps he simply told you what you wanted to hear."

"No!" said Kit. "I know it's true."

"Mmm hmmm," Valker mumbled through his bound beak.

"Our historians have written often of these so-called zoos," said Uncle Rik. "And while they do exist, our kind has always been safe from them. They are not like the jails where wild dogs and cats are sometimes taken. They are more like playhouses for the People's entertainment. They lock animal folk up and stare at them. Why would People want to lock raccoons and squirrels away in cages to stare at when we share the alleys behind their homes with them already? It makes no sense, Kit."

"But People don't make sense!" Kit replied. He felt bad yelling at his uncle, who was just trying to keep him from being disappointed, but he couldn't bear to think of giving up on his mother before he'd even had a chance to look for her. It was all he'd thought about all winter and now it seemed he had a real chance at finding her! "People don't do things for good reasons like us animal folk," he said. "You taught me that yourself!"

"I know you have your hopes of seeing your mother again set high," Uncle Rik said. "She is my sister and I dream of seeing her again too. But to go chasing after her in a zoo? No, Kit. It's not possible. Our kind don't get put in zoos. The People . . ." He tensed. "They get rid of us in other ways. More . . . *terrible* ways."

The animals all looked at their paws on the floor or the ceiling of the saloon. The chickens shivered and hugged their wings against their bodies. The mice rubbed their necks, and even the Blacktail brothers coughed nervously. Every alley creature of fur or feather was scared of getting taken away by the People or of getting snapped up by one of their traps. Every alley creature had lost a friend or family member to People's traps at one time or another.

"Does no one here care about our neighbors, then?" Kit pleaded. "Does no one here know what *howl to snap* means? It's not the howl that we're born with or the snap of the trap that takes us out that matters. It's what we do in between that howl and that snap! You all taught me that! I want the space between my howl and that snap to matter. I want to be someone who keeps his promises and who helps folks who need it! Dax and his mother are gone! And the Liney sisters and Sebastian and those two old squirrels whose names I can't remember but who were probably really nice or maybe they weren't nice but that shouldn't matter—"

"Kit," Eeni whispered. "Wind it up . . . you're losing them."

Kit slouched. He was no good at speeches. "I just thought we looked after our own in Ankle Snap Alley," he said. "I guess I was wrong."

Eeni put her paw on his back to comfort him. "You all should be ashamed of yourselves. You're selfish, cowardly folk, and you aren't worth the sneeze of a flea in Kit's fur. You don't have the right to scold him or to tell him what to do." She stepped up to the hawk tied to the counter and started to tear the knots that held him. "Come on," she said. "Let it never be said the Moonlight Brigade breaks its promises."

In a flash, the hawk burst free of his tethers and cast a vicious gaze around the room. All the little creatures tensed. He narrowed his eyes at Eeni, unsure if he should eat her for tricking him or thank her for freeing him. But he was terribly outnumbered and terribly confused, so he flew out with one mighty beat of his wings and left the little animals standing in silent shock behind him.

"There!" said Eeni. "What's done is done. He's gone." She turned to Kit, and the rest of the Moonlight Brigade stood with her. "Now let's get out of here and investigate this place called the zoo ourselves. We don't need all these scared scurrying scalawags to help us anyway. We're the Moonlight Brigade and no one tells us what to do!"

They all turned to leave together with Kit, but Blue Neck Ned flapped in front of them, blocking the door. "Oh no you don't!" he yelled. "You don't storm out on us after what you did, letting that hawk go! We storm out on you!"

Eeni rolled her eyes, but let Ned turn and storm out through the door first. Kit looked back over his shoulder at the adult animals.

Uncle Rik looked so sad, like he wanted to help Kit but just couldn't bring himself to hope that Kit would actually find his mother.

And Mr. Timinson looked like he wanted to help but couldn't defy the rest of Ankle Snap Alley because they paid his teacher salary.

The others looked away from Kit because they knew they were wrong to scold him for keeping his word and they knew they were wrong to criticize him for wanting to find his mother, but they also knew they weren't brave enough to help, so they looked down at their paws and claws in shame.

Kit shook his head at the whole sorry scene, and had turned to leave Larkanon's when he heard a terrible squawk from outside, followed by the ringing of high-pitched bells.

Everyone rushed for the door and out into the sunlight. It was morning. They'd been arguing about Valker most of the night and they hadn't noticed new traps being set outside.

But right there in the center of the alley was Blue Neck Ned, flapping his wings furiously, but not getting anywhere because his ankles were snared in a trap.

Chapter Three

QUICK OF PAW

BLUE Neck Ned panicked. His wings beat uselessly against the air and he tugged and pulled on the cord that held him to the ground. With every flap, the knot around his ankle drew tighter and tiny little bells on the trap rang out. The ringing bells made the Flealess dogs in the houses all around Ankle Snap Alley bark and howl.

"Quiet, Ned!" Kit warned. He rushed across the alley to Ned's side and started working his clever fingers over the trap. He was a raccoon of some trap-springing skill, but couldn't do much with Ned's wings flapping in his face. "Stay calm and I'll get you out!"

"I'm trapped! I'm trapped!" Ned shouted, not staying calm at all. "They're coming for me! They'll take me for sure! I'm too pretty to be in a zoo!"

"Quiet, feather face!" Eeni scolded him. "You'll call down every Person in the whole city on us!"

Kit found the bottom of the trap buried below the dirt of the alley. There was a stake in the ground with a loop of rope on a spring tied to it. Ned had set the spring off when he'd stepped on a hidden switch and the string had zipped itself tight around his ankles. The string was made out of a kind of People material, the same stuff they used to make the bags that always got stuck in trees—plastic. He couldn't loosen it and he couldn't break it.

"Work faster, Kit!" Ned yelled. Kit looked up and saw that all the house pets were at the windows, howling like mad to get their People's attention. He heard one voice above all the others, even through the window, the miniature greyhound, Titus, leader of the Flealess and sworn enemy of all Wild Ones, most of all Kit.

"It's that nasty raccoon!" the dog shouted. "He's attacking a pigeon! It looks like he's got Foaming Mouth Fever! You should put him down!"

The dog winked at Kit from behind the glass. Though the dog's People couldn't understand him, it was still a nasty thing to say. You didn't joke at a raccoon about Foaming Mouth Fever. Foaming Mouth Fever had ended the lives of many noble raccoons, and it was a sensitive subject.

Kit scowled and focused again on setting Ned free. He couldn't get the plastic cord off Ned's ankle, so he had to wriggle his little claw into the knot and try to untie it from the stake. He worked at the knot, twisting and loosening, then trying to chew it with his teeth. The other animals watched in amazement. Kit hadn't yet found a trap he couldn't undo.

Well, except for one . . . the one that had trapped his mother all those seasons ago.

"You got it, Kit," Eeni whispered in encouragement. "But maybe get it faster?"

His ears perked and twisted in the direction of the far end of the alley. Faintly, he heard the *screech* of brakes and the *crunch* of tires. He turned to see that one of those rolling boxes that People rode around in—a car—had pulled up outside the alley. This was a big square car and Kit's instincts screamed at him that it was bad news. A wise raccoon would listen to his instincts and run away. The People inside the car got out and headed straight for the alley.

"Scatter!" Rocks barked.

"Run!" Shane and Flynn Blacktail cried.

"Don't leave me, Kit!" Blue Neck Ned squawked.

Kit was kinder than he was wise. He stayed and kept fidgeting with the trap. "Almost got it," he said, his tongue poking out the side of his mouth as he concentrated. Eeni kept looking back at the approaching people, who had bags and crates and nets with them.

"This doesn't look good, Kit," she said. "I think these are the People who've been scooping everyone up."

"Kit?" his uncle Rik added. "We really must get out of here now."

"Squawk! Squawk! Squawk!" cried Blue Neck Ned. "Don't leave me!"

The People drew closer. Out of the corner of his eye, Kit saw them point at him, heard them say something to each other in their language. Heard their footsteps getting nearer and nearer.

"Got it!" he cheered as the plastic cord slipped from the spring. Ned leaped away, flapping into the air.

"Oh, thank you, Kit!" the pigeon cried. "I won't forget what you've done for me!"

"Yeah, right," Eeni grumbled. "I bet he's already forgotten."

"Let's go!" Kit said, and he turned to run away with Eeni, but something was wrong. Uncle Rik wasn't following them.

Kit stopped, looked back, and saw his uncle standing

still, just a few steps from where Ned had been trapped.

"I'm sorry, Kit," said Uncle Rik, pointing down at his own leg. A trap had snapped around *his* ankles. And the People were nearly on top of him.

"Go," he said. "There is no time. Hide."

"But—" Kit took a step in his direction, eyes darting to the trap. It was the same kind that had trapped Ned. He could undo it if he had time.

"Eeni, we need to distract those People," Kit said.

"How?" she asked.

"We could . . . um . . ." Kit had no ideas. His mind was jumbled. Even while he was standing there looking at his uncle, his brain had pushed him backward in time, to the memory of his last moments with his mother. She was caught in a trap a lot like this one. A pack of hunting dogs was bearing down on her and Kit couldn't set her free.

He tried to get out of the memory, but when he looked at Uncle Rik and the People walking toward him, he saw his mother and the hunting dogs too. Sometimes seeing his mother's face in his memory made him smile, but not right now. Why did memory sometimes act like a cool swimming hole and sometimes like a pit of quicksand?

Kit had panicked when he'd lost his mother, but he was younger then, two seasons younger. Now that he was the leader of the Moonlight Brigade, he would not panic.

"Get the finches to raise a ruckus," Kit told Eeni. "We

can send them swooping down to drive the People back."

"Kit," Eeni said. "The finches are hiding. *Everyone* is hiding. Everyone but us."

"Then we'll do this ourselves," Kit said, and took another step toward his trapped uncle.

The People could clearly see him, just as he could clearly see them. They wore matching beige uniforms with hats on their heads and big heavy brown shoes on their feet. It amazed Kit how much People dressed like animals—except for the shoes, of course. Animal folk would never put on shoes. People didn't notice how much they were just like the animal folk, didn't pay any attention to their clothes or stores and definitely didn't learn their language. People thought the wild world was theirs and they were the only ones who mattered in it.

But Kit wasn't about to let them get away with it, not this time.

"Don't worry, Uncle Rik, I'm going to get you out of this trap. There're no paws faster than mine when it comes to springing traps."

"No, Kit," said Uncle Rik. "You need to run. You don't have time. I'm an old raccoon and the alley will be fine without me. But you . . . they *need* you, Kit."

"But *I* need *you*, Uncle Rik," Kit said.

"Please, do what I ask, and go," his uncle said. The People had stopped nearby and were watching them.

Kit turned and looked at the People, hesitated. He even thought about charging at them with his claws out, hissing and barking every curse word he could think of. They wouldn't understand him, but they'd at least know he was angry. Even clueless People could tell what a fella meant when he showed his fangs.

But he never got the chance.

"Go right now!" Uncle Rik shouted, showing his own fangs. It made Kit jump.

He and Eeni scurried beneath the nearby Dumpster and watched in horror as the People shoved Uncle Rik into a crate. They didn't even notice he'd lost his robe and glasses. People never noticed that sort of thing. They just set their traps and took what they wanted.

Kit seethed beneath the Dumpster, hot anger burning from the tip of his tail to the points of his whiskers. They'd trapped his mother and taken her from him and now they'd trapped his uncle too? No! He wouldn't have it.

"What are you doing, Kit?" Eeni saw him creeping forward. "The People aren't gone yet."

"I know," said Kit. "That's why I'm slipping out."

"What?"

"I'm going to follow them," Kit said. "And I'm going to get my uncle back. If they're really taking him to the *zoo*, then I'm going to get all the other animals back too. And my mother. You can help or not, but I swear from howl to snap that I am doing this. You with me?"

"You know I'm with you," Eeni answered. "Howl to snap."

Kit smiled at his friend, and then raced out from underneath the Dumpster without looking over his shoulder to check if Eeni was with him. She was his best friend. He knew she'd be right by his side.

For the first time in either of their lives, the rat and the raccoon weren't being chased by People. They were the ones doing the chasing.

Chapter Four

TAKEN FOR
A RIDE

BY the time the People loaded Uncle Rik's crate into the back of their car and got inside the front, Kit and Eeni had caught up to them and were huddled just behind the metal beast, out of sight. The car made a roaring noise and belched something black and stinky from its behind, right into Kit's and Eeni's faces.

"Ugh, gross!" Eeni groaned. "What do they feed this thing?"

Kit had no idea, but he wasn't really worried about what People fed their cars. He was worried about how he was going to follow one. He wished he had more of a plan, because when you've got a best friend trusting you, you owe them your very best plan. But for now, any sort of plan would have to do.

He scanned the trash-strewn alley and his eyes settled on the rusty bicycle wheel that had been lying in the dirt for as long as Kit had lived there.

He ran to it and dragged it behind the car.

"Help me balance this," he asked Eeni, who scurried underneath it and heaved it up on her back. Kit lifted it by the spokes from the other side until the wheel was standing upright. Eeni steadied it while Kit jumped on, setting his back paws on the hub of the wheel and gripping around it with his nimble toes. His front paws grabbed the rear bumper of the car.

The wheel wobbled and Kit nearly toppled sideways, but he held himself up. He'd invented a unicycle.

Now he just had to ride it.

Eeni looked up at him and shook her head. "You're crazier than a hummingbird in a hurricane."

The car shuddered and began to roll forward, and Kit's wheel turned beneath him. His paws started to slip from the back of the car, so he dug his sharp claws into the hard plastic bumper. It made a terrible noise and made his palms hurt with the effort, but he was moving now, being towed behind the People's car.

The car pulled out of the entrance to Ankle Snap Alley toward the great river of pavement the People called a road.

"Come on!" Kit called down to Eeni. She ran after him as fast she could, her white fur lit red by the rear lights of the car. "Jump!"

Just as the car sped up, Eeni leaped and caught Kit's long bushy tail. The car turned and she nearly lost hold as she swung out sideways, but she dug her claws in and held on.

"Ow!" Kit yelled.

"Sorry," Eeni replied, climbing up his back to perch in the fur on his shoulder. It took all Kit's focus to keep the wheel balanced upright as the car went faster and faster. The pavement raced below the deflated tire that spun with a *thump thump thump*.

"Ahh!" Kit yelled, while the car snaked its way into high-speed traffic. Every bump and crack in the road made them bounce and jump.

Kit teetered on the wheel and thought for sure he'd fall.

"Don't let go!" Eeni shouted into his ear.

"I won't if you won't!" he replied.

Kit's claws ached and the strong wind rushed through his fur, while the stink of fumes from the car stung his nose and eyes. His back paws burned against the wheel below and it took all the strength in his legs to keep his wobbly unicycle balanced. He didn't know how long he could keep going like this.

Suddenly, another car zoomed up behind them, flashing lights from its front end. It honked and honked and Kit looked over his shoulder to see one of the People in the car pointing at him.

"I think they see us," he shouted at Eeni over the loud honking.

"Why are they making that terrible noise?" she wondered.

"I guess they're not used to actually seeing us?" Kit said as the car behind them sped up and moved around. A group of young People in the backseat gawked at Kit and Eeni. That was when Eeni did something Kit had not expected: she stuck out her tongue.

The People in the car yelled something over at the People from the zoo and Kit's stomach twisted in knots as the car slowed and pulled to the side, rolling to a stop while other cars zoomed past them.

"Why'd they stop?" Eeni wondered.

"They know we're here!" Kit cried, and let go of the bumper. He jumped off the wheel and let it clatter to the ground. At the same instant, they heard the car doors open and the People get out.

"Quick, go underneath!" Eeni tugged his fur like she was steering him. He took the signal and dove underneath the car, curling behind one of the big car tires and holding his breath as the People's brown shoes strolled around to the back. One of them picked up the old bicycle wheel and said something to the other one. It sounded like a question because the voice rose at the end of the sentence. Kit strained to make out any words that were the same in their language and his, but he couldn't make heads or tails of their words. He couldn't believe People actually made sense of all the weird sounds they made at one another.

The People stood there for ages, until finally, they left the bicycle wheel where it was and got back into their car.

The machine rumbled and shuddered and began to move again, slowly pointing its nose back onto the road. He had to find something to hold on to, and fast!

He reached up to grab a pole on the underside of the car, but it was scorching hot and he barked in pain when he touched it. He tried something else but it was spinning so fast it nearly shaved the skin off his paw.

"It's dangerous under here!" he cried.

"We gotta go up," Eeni said. "To the roof!"

As the car rolled forward, exposing Kit and Eeni to the sunlight overhead, they scampered up onto the rear bumper and waited until the exact moment that the car heaved itself into traffic and zoomed forward. The People were paying so much attention ahead, they didn't notice the raccoon and the rat scramble over their rear window and scurry onto their roof.

The moment his claws scritch-scratched across the roof, Kit wished they were still riding a unicycle off the back. It was one thing to be up high—Kit didn't mind heights at all—but it was another thing to be up high and moving faster than any animal was meant to move, with nothing but your claw tips and a prayer to the First Raccoon to keep you from falling under the wheels of the rushing cars all around.

Kit spread his arms and legs out wide and pressed his belly flat against the roof. He lowered his head so he didn't have to see how fast they were going. Still, he could hear the *screech* and *honk* of the cars and feel the *thump* of the road rumbling below. This was *not* how a raccoon was meant to travel.

"Kit, look up, you're missing it! This is amazing!" Eeni cheered, clinging to the fur on his back with her tail flapping like a banner behind her. "Is this really how People get around? If I had a car I'd never use my legs again! Woohoo!"

Kit looked up and immediately wished he hadn't. Buildings whooshed by on either side of them while smaller cars zipped past, and Kit shuddered, imagining his bones pulverized underneath their tires. He slammed his eyes shut again, but still he felt the car racing along, taking him farther and farther from Ankle Snap Alley, and deeper and deeper into the unknown corners of the city, to places where People ruled and wild animals did their best to disappear. Kit really wanted to disappear.

"Kit!" Eeni tugged at his fur. "We need to disappear!"

Kit opened one eye and then the other. Eeni had a way of plucking the thoughts from his head and speaking them aloud. She was an expert at that particular kind of friend-magic.

The car had stopped. They were at a big gate, and a person in a blue uniform was opening it for the car to go through. Kit pressed himself as flat as he could against the rooftop, and Eeni scurried off his back and slid underneath him. Luckily, the Person didn't bother looking up.

The metal of the gate squealed as it opened and Kit studied it as the car passed through. The iron bars were bent and twisted into the shapes of trees and animals. Kit's nose picked up scents of flowers and grasses. He also smelled animals—deer and wolf and wild dog. There were water smells too, fish and salt and beaver fur. These weren't city smells at all; these were Big Sky smells, smells from the wild world beyond the city, the world Kit had come from. The world he never thought he'd see again.

Those smells didn't belong here.

"I think we're inside the zoo," Kit told Eeni, and then he shuddered. As the car crept forward, he smelled another smell, one any animal who hopes to live past suckling age learns to catch on even the faintest breeze.

He smelled fear.

Chapter Five

A QUESTION
OF THE Q

THE People drove and drove along winding roads, and Kit marveled at the way they had built a fake forest in the middle of the city, and beside the forest, a fake grassland, and a fake riverbank. There was a giant cage filled with trees and inside it, Kit heard birds singing their songs of sadness.

> *Ohhhh, my feathers are for flying*
> *And ohhhh, my feathers grow and grow.*
> *Ohhhh, the sky is high above me*

And ohhhh, I'm down here below.
Oh, oh, oh, when will I ever go?
Oh, oh, oh, does the wind still blow and blow?

"They can see the sky," Eeni gasped, and squeezed tighter on Kit's fur as the mournful song rose. "But they can't fly to it."

Kit looked from the giant birdcage to a large pond behind a low fence. There were benches set up along the fence so People could look at the pond from one side. The other side was blocked off from view by plants and trees that Kit didn't recognize. It was a pond from somewhere else, a pond that should have reflected a different sky.

The whole place was a theater set, but instead of telling the ancient stories of the animal folk who lived and spoke with People, like real plays did, the People had made a pretend version of the world as it was now, and somewhere in it all, they'd trapped the animals.

"Is this a dream?" Eeni asked.

"More like a nightmare," Kit said. "Uncle Rik said the zoo wasn't a jail, but it sure looks like one to me."

The car pulled up to a squat brick building and the People got out—without looking up to the rooftop either—and opened the car's back doors. Kit saw his uncle huddled in the dark cage, shaking with fright. Uncle Rik's eyes instantly darted up in Kit's direction.

They went wide when he saw his nephew and he shook his head no.

Kit knew Uncle Rik didn't want him to endanger himself with some daring rescue, but he also must have known that Kit was not going to let Uncle Rik get kidnapped. He didn't dare make a noise, but he wanted to tell his uncle it would be all right, so he put his claws together with his thumb tips touching in the middle to make the symbol of Azban, the First Raccoon, founder of the Moonlight Brigade and Trickster Prince of the wild world.

He felt pretty cool every time he did it.

The People hauled the crate away and disappeared inside the building. The last thing Kit saw was his uncle Rik, still shaking his head at Kit, warning him not to do anything risky, but *risky* was Kit's middle name.

Actually, he didn't have a middle name, but if he did, he'd want it to be something as cool as "Risky."

Only when Kit was sure the People were gone did he and Eeni climb down from the roof of the car. They scurried over to the bushes that ran along the outside of the building, looking for a way to sneak in. All the doors and all the windows were closed. Eeni found a good rat hole, but it had been stuffed with metal wire to keep rodents out.

"These People know what they're doing," she said. "This building's sealed tighter than a dog's nose at a skunk parade."

"Since when do skunks parade?" Kit asked, although he knew better than to question one of Eeni's sayings. She just liked making them up. They didn't have to make sense as long as they sounded true. "We have to find a way in," Kit said, sitting back on his haunches to wrangle his thoughts together. Eeni sat beside him, wrangling her own thoughts.

Neither of their thoughts were so easily wrangled.

"Oh, my dear darling flea-bitten fellows, you are quite far from home, aren't you?" The lilting voice of a bright peacock interrupted them as he strutted around the corner of the building, calm as could be, his broad-plumed tail flowing out like a gown behind him. "I should warn you to hide yourselves, and yet I am so very curious what brought you here all the way from"—the peacock paused and looked them up and down with the eye on one side of his head—"Ankle Snap Alley, yes?"

"How did you know that?" Kit asked.

"Oh, a peacock like myself knows how to size up friend and foe alike with a glance," the peacock said. "I can see by your clothes that you come from a place where People pay you no attention, and I can see from the dirt on your claws that you're the sort who doesn't care much for appearances either. And of course, it is plain as the daylight above us that you belong beneath the moon, not our bright daytime sun. So I asked myself, what would bring two filthy-clothed tricksters, awake in the daylight, all the way here to our peaceful zoo?"

"We're here to—" Kit began, but the peacock wasn't interested in Kit's response. He had an answer to his own question already.

"You are here to find your friends from Ankle Snap Alley," he said.

Kit and Eeni nodded together.

The peacock fluffed his bright feathers, preening, proud of himself.

"Do you know where they are?" Kit asked him.

"I know everything about this place," the peacock said. "My name is Preston Q Brightfeather the Second, eldest son of Preston Q Brightfeather the First, Squire of the Great Order of Peacocks, and Captain of the Southeast Corridor of the Zoo."

"That is a long name," Eeni observed. "What's the *Q* stand for?"

"Rat! How dare you insult my father's middle initial! The *Q* does not *stand* for anything!" the peacock hissed. "A peacock's initial stands only for itself! To stand for anything else would be beneath its dignity! I should never have assumed such alley trash was worth my time!"

The bird began to turn away, but Kit called out to stop him.

"Sorry to offend you and your—uh—glorious middle initial." Kit tried to make peace. He added a little bow to his apology on Eeni's behalf because he'd figured out right away this peacock needed to feel superior, and it cost Kit nothing to let him. "We would be most honored if you'd show us where our friends from Ankle Snap Alley are. I know they are nothing but dirty crooked liars and alley-trash-eating cheats, but they're our friends nonetheless and we'd love to find them. You, noble peacock, are the only one who can help us."

"Hrmpf," said the peacock, still angry at the accidental insult Eeni had given him, but Kit's humility and praise worked its way into his heart and he relented. With a polite bow of his plumed head, the peacock smiled gently. "Very well, follow me."

They walked after the peacock, following his strutting steps on a path around the building to a window by the front door.

The peacock stopped and looked to the large metal gates across an open courtyard from the building. "Climb up and have yourselves a look," he said. "But be quick." He pointed his claw at a Person in the distance, walking around to check all the locks. "The zoo People do a final check to make sure the animals are secure just before they open for the day. Once that one is done checking, the People will flood this place full. You *do not* want to be here when they do."

"Thanks," said Kit, following the peacock's gaze to the spot at the entrance where a large group of young People were lining up to enter. Kit turned around and stretched up his paws to reach the window ledge, then began a straining pull-up to bring his chin above the sill, where he could see inside.

"Brace yourself," Preston warned. "I believe what you are about to see might smash your senses to smithereens."

"I've seen a lot in my time," Kit said. "I think I can handle whatever is on the other side of this—"

He never finished his sentence because what he saw through the glass had smashed his senses to smithereens.

Chapter Six

WEIRD WINDOWS

"LET me up there to see," Eeni said to Kit, scurrying up his tail like a ladder and climbing onto his head to look for herself.

When she saw, she gasped and nearly fell down his face. She had to grip his ears for support.

"Ow!" Kit yelped, which brought him back to himself.

"Are you seeing what I'm seeing?" Eeni asked him.

Kit nodded, which nearly knocked Eeni off his head again, but he still couldn't find the words to describe what was on the other side of the window in the zoo building.

There was a big open area of floor and in front of it were three huge windows that went from the floor to the ceiling and were even wider across. The windows didn't look outside, though, at least not to the outside that was outside this building.

One window was filled with water and fish swam on the other side of it. It was like a window to the underside of a river. Kit had never seen so many different kinds of fish so clearly before. He'd jumped in rivers as a little child in the forest beneath the big sky, and he scooped fish from the rivers for dinner, but he'd never just seen them swimming calmly in their endless blue circles. It was beautiful to see and yet unsettling.

The window beside the fish looked out on a desert. The People had made it look like the desert went on forever to the horizon, but it was a trick of their art. The People who'd made this fake desert were skillful, but still, a keen eye could see it was false.

But the animal folk inside were not false. They were real creatures of a kind Kit didn't recognize. They had long furry bodies and little black-and-white faces. They looked something like weasels, but like no weasels Kit had ever met before. There were three of them. One was sleeping, one was doing little push-ups, and one was staring off into the fake horizon.

But it wasn't the fish or the desert weasels that had

made Kit fall speechless. It was what he saw in the third window. It was Ankle Snap Alley.

Somehow, the People had built a model of Kit's home. There was Possum Ansel's bakery—although it was missing its sign—and there were the Gnarly Oak Apartments where Kit lived, but only part of them. He saw the Dancing Squirrel Theater, but it had no stage or curtains, and the Dumpster Market where the scavengers traded goods, and the old van where the Rabid Rascals lived, and even the big stone slab of the Reptile Bank and Trust. Everything was there, but in smaller size, and parts were only painted on, just like the horizon in the desert next door. The People hadn't gotten it totally right; they'd created the space but not the feel of the place. It looked even more false than the painted desert.

But inside, sitting by a broken bicycle wheel that was painted to look old and rusted but still had shiny new parts, was Dax the squirrel, nibbling a peanut, while his mother napped beside him. And there were the Liney sisters and one of the gecko bankers and a news finch Kit hadn't even known had been taken, and then his eye lingered on the narrow space where Enrique Gallo's Fur Styling Shop and Barbería should have been. Instead of the shop, the People had put a fake trash can and on top of the trash can was a big lump of gray-and-black fur, curled up to sleep for the day, and even though he couldn't see the lump's face, he knew it was a raccoon and he knew just the raccoon it was.

"Mom?" he said out loud, his voice caught in his throat like a mouse in a trap.

She couldn't hear him.

He tried to think so hard in her direction that she'd wake up and look his way, but thoughts didn't work like that and all he managed to do was make his eyes tear up and his head go spinning dizzy.

"They call it *the Urban Wild*," Preston Q Bright-feather called up to them. "A new show for the People, highlighting the animal life of the city that they think is theirs."

"But . . . that's my mother!" Kit shouted. "She never even lived in Ankle Snap Alley! They have my mother! My uncle *and* my mother! They're my whole family! I have to get them out!"

He scratched at the glass.

"Calm down, child," the peacock told him. "Look around this place. They have a lot of folks' mothers and uncles. You'll never get them out by throwing a fit. They're locked in tight."

Kit took a deep breath and looked at the glass wall again, searching for a locked door into the Urban Wild cage. Kit had yet to find a lock he could not pick open, but he couldn't even see one here. Inside the cage, along the back wall, there was an outline of a door, painted like the rest of the wall so it was almost invisible. It didn't have a lock that he could see, though, just a little box next to it with a bunch of buttons and symbols on it. He had no idea what sort of lock that was.

"I need to break them out!" he cried.

"You won't get them out now, Kit," the peacock told him. "The People are the only ones who know how to use those locks, and not even all of them know how. But they will have you locked up too if you don't get moving."

The peacock pointed to the front gates of the zoo as they opened and a herd of People rushed in, mostly the People's children, with a few full-grown ones mixed in, shouting and pointing. The herd stampeded straight for the building where Kit was hanging off the ledge.

He and Eeni dropped into the bushes below the window and hid.

"You can get out behind this building," Preston told them. "Follow the path through the false forest and you'll reach a fence. From there, you're on your own."

"But I can't leave!" Kit cried. "I need to figure out that strange lock and free my family!"

"Kit." Eeni put her paw on his. "We can't rescue them right now, not with all these People here. We have to do what we do best. We have to make a plan and we have to get help. We have to go back home."

"Your friend is right," said the peacock. "There is nothing you can do right now. Your family and your friends are part of the show. And as the great bird poet William Shakesparrow once said, *The show must go on.* Go home, child. Plan your plans. These People are cleverer than you think, but you have a friend in me. No one knows the zoo better than Preston Q Brightfeather and I will help you set your friends and family free from the Urban Wild."

Kit hesitated. He wasn't used to trusting strange birds and he was in shock from seeing his mother alive after all this time. But then he nodded. "Thank you."

"No need to thank me," said the bird. "I'll be happy to see your kind on its way from my zoo. They are not meant to be here after all. We are a place for magnificent animals who fill the world with beauty and grace, not animals who"—he looked Kit and Eeni up and down with one side eye—"*scurry*," he sneered.

Then the bird strutted out from behind the bush and raised his tail feathers, spreading them out in a glorious fan of color. The young People *oohed* and *aahed* at the peacock. Kit and Eeni tried to decide if the bird's offer to help them was worth accepting his insult, but the bird glanced back at them and screeched, "Go, you fools, or they'll put you in the cages too!"

Kit and Eeni ran.

No one paid any attention to the flash of grimy

gray-and-white fur as a rat and a raccoon slipped away around the back of the building. Preston had caused enough of a distraction for the two of them to escape, but it would take more than a flash of fabulous feathers to break Kit's mother and his uncle Rik, and all the other kidnapped creatures of Ankle Snap Alley, out of that cage.

If he was going to pull off a breakout like that, Kit was going to need to come up with a plan as clever as any raccoon ever had since the days of Azban, the First Raccoon. And to do that, he was going to need to get some help from some animals who were surely in no mood to help him after he'd set that hawk free.

His neighbors in Ankle Snap Alley.

Chapter Seven

FOLLOW THE LEADER(S)

"SO you're saying they're in a play?" Possum Ansel asked as he served Kit and Eeni a cola-can custard with eggshell and lemon-peel sprinkles. The sun had set and Possum Ansel's bakery was full of customers, all of them eager to hear what Kit and Eeni had seen at the zoo, even though none of them had been eager to risk their own necks going there.

"It's not a play." Kit tried to explain the zoo to Ansel and his customers. "It's like the scenery in a play, but they're trying to make it look like real life."

"You can tell, though," Eeni added with her mouth full of custard. She had a gob of it on the tip of her little pink nose and she licked it off before she continued. "Nothing looks quite right. The colors are too bright and the background is too shallow. You can tell People painted it, not animal folk. People just don't have the rodents' gift for making art."

"Their artistry is not our concern!" said Martyn to a chorus of agreement from the church mice behind him. "What are they doing with our neighbors? They have no right to take our kind into their zoos! The Moonlight Brigade exists to prevent just this sort of calamity!"

"Hey!" Eeni objected. "I didn't hear any of *you* offering to help us when we went to the zoo, so now that we're back, why don't you let us eat our custard in peace before haranguing us!"

Kit smirked a little. *Haranguing* was just a fancy way of saying *scolding*, but Eeni never missed a chance to show those mice she knew just as many big words as they did.

It had taken him and Eeni the rest of the daylight just to make it back to Ankle Snap Alley on foot. They'd had to keep to the shadows and the side streets, because if a Person saw them, they knew they'd be snatched up. If they were, they'd have been *lucky* to be locked in the zoo. Uncle Rik was right when he'd told Kit what usually happened to folks like them when the People caught them.

Most of the time, alley folk like them who got snatched up in the daylight were never seen again.

Kit took a bite of custard while the church mice shifted from paw to paw with impatience. He wasn't actually hungry, he just wasn't ready to talk to everyone yet. He was still angry at them for yelling at him about letting Valker go free. And the sight of his mother in the People's zoo had robbed him of his appetite. All winter long, he'd wondered how he would find her again and what sort of place a zoo might be, but now that he knew, he could not imagine how he would get her out.

He needed the time it took to swallow his custard to think. Twice now, he'd had all of Ankle Snap Alley crowded around him making demands without offering any solutions themselves.

When he became the leader of the Moonlight Brigade, he had thought it would be all planning tricks and capers and heists, leading raids and being cheered by grateful creatures, large and small. He hadn't realized how much being a leader was just explaining stuff to impatient crowds. Mr. Timinson wasn't even there to help out. He'd gone off to wherever foxes went when they weren't teaching classes. A library, maybe, or a henhouse?

"I'm going to get our neighbors out," he told everyone in the bakery. "I just don't know how yet." Everyone gasped, although they shouldn't have been surprised. He hadn't had a moment to think since his uncle was taken.

"Relax," Eeni reassured them all. "Not-knowing is just the first place you put your paws on the path to knowing. Wouldn't be much point to sniffing the wind if you already knew what it'd smell like before it blew by."

The creatures of Ankle Snap Alley murmured their agreement with Eeni's wisdom, even the ones who didn't really understand what she meant, because she'd said it with such confidence. That was another trick of leadership Kit wished he had: a way with words. He wasn't half the talker Eeni was, but then again, she wasn't half the plotter he was. Together the two of them made *one* pretty good leader.

"Here's what I'm going to do," Kit said, shoving in one more mouthful of Possum Ansel's gooey cola custard. "A heist is like breaking open a beaver dam. If you can find the weak spot in the dam, you can let all the water come rushing out. We just have to find the weak spot in the zoo."

"So you'll have to go *back* there?" Blue Neck Ned cooed.

"You couldn't pay me to go back there," Shane Blacktail said.

"But you've never been there a first time, brother, so how could you go back?" Flynn Blacktail replied.

"Well, no one paid me to go a first time either!" Shane

explained. "A raccoon with sense doesn't risk his fur for free anytime."

"And yet Kit's risking more than his fur to set his friends and family free," said Flynn.

"He's sentimental," said Shane.

"You can't spell *sentimental* without *mental*," said Flynn.

"Neither of you can spell at all," Eeni cut them off. "And if you're not offering to help, you might as well shut your snouts. I've never heard creatures talk more and say less than you two Blacktail brothers!"

Shane and Flynn growled at her, but she growled right back. A rat's growl sounded more like a squeak, but Eeni's squeak was backed by smarts and both the brothers knew it. They went quiet.

"The Moonlight Brigade will go back to the zoo together tomorrow night," Kit said. "We've got an ally there, a peacock who will help us. We'll learn everything we can about the place and then . . ." He paused and glanced around the bakery. Every animal, in all their shapes and sizes, was looking to him, afraid and uncertain. He took a deep breath and told them what he thought they'd want to hear. "Then we'll make the People regret they ever messed with Ankle Snap Alley."

Fanged grins spread around the room. Kit knew how

much better it felt to feel powerful than to feel afraid. He had no plan yet nor any idea how he was going to keep his promise to raid the zoo and break out the folks trapped in the Urban Wild exhibit, but he knew his neighborhood needed to hear his confidence so that's what he gave them.

"Beware!" A loud voice shook Possum Ansel's as a shadow darkened the doorway. "What you bite will not be what you chew, and what you chew may be more than you have bitten."

Kit turned with all the other animals to see the form that spoke from outside. It was not one voice speaking in a riddle, but a hundred speaking together as one, not one creature, but a hundred tangled rats who lived as one.

It was the Rat King.

Chapter Eight

OF CABBAGES AND KINGS

MOST folks could go their whole lives without ever seeing the Rat King, and yet here the Rat King was, come from their mysterious hideaway to speak to all of Ankle Snap Alley at once. As far as Kit knew, this had never happened before, not even in the ancient days of the First Animals.

"Uh, hi," said Eeni, who lost her wordy wit when it came to the Rat King. Somewhere in that tangle of a hundred rats was her mother, who'd left her long ago to tangle her tail and surrender herself within the Rat King. It was a noble calling to become one of the hundred rats, but once a creature joined, she never left. She was like a tear dropped into the ocean, adding its salt to the sea.

Eeni's mother lived, but Eeni was an orphan nonetheless.

At the sight of the Rat King in his doorway, Possum Ansel immediately rushed back into the kitchen, dragging Otis the badger with him. "The Rat King! *Here!* In my bakery! "What do we cook for *royalty*?!" The sound of pots and pans banging and rattling broke the stunned silence of the rest of the animals.

The mice bowed; Blue Neck Ned yelped and flew to the back corner farthest from the door, and all the other creatures clucked and cooed and started asking questions.

"What does my future hold?" a weasel wanted to know.

"Will we be rich?" wondered the Blacktail brothers.

"Is the moon made of stinky cheese or of a subtle cheddar?" wondered Martyn the church mouse.

Everyone believed the Rat King was all-knowing and all-seeing, but really, the Rat King just saw one hundred times more than any one animal and thought one hundred times more thoughts than any one animal. Kit knew it wasn't magic that made the Rat King powerful. It was perspective.

"Silence!" the Rat King commanded, and the silence returned. "We have not come from our seclusion to be questioned about your quibbles. We have come to tell you that the wild world is not all of one mind, nor do all paws and claws wish to scratch the same dirt. There are as many truths as teeth and it is the ones you do not see that bite. Beware."

The Rat King's words hung heavy in the air and then, as if they themselves were one creature with many heads, every furred and feathered face in the bakery turned to look at Kit.

"Does the Rat King always speak in riddles?" the rooster, Enrique, wanted to know.

"I thought they could tell the future," the chicken Mrs. Costlecrunk declared.

"What *are* they blabbering about?" Blue Neck Ned squawked from his perch, still staying as far away from the Rat King as possible.

"What you bite will not be what you chew, and what you chew may be more than you have bitten," repeated the Rat King.

"Yeah, like that," Enrique said. "Riddles. Are we supposed to solve the riddles?"

"No," Eeni grumbled. "The Rat King just likes to confuse us so we'll think they're wise."

"But they are wise!" Martyn said, still with his head bowed. The church mice had great respect for the Rat King. None of the other folks in Ankle Snap Alley seemed to.

"Chewing more than you can bite don't sound like wisdom to me," said Blue Neck Ned.

"They don't get it," said one rat in the Rat King to another. Unlike someone made up of only themselves, someone who was made up of a hundred someones had to say their thoughts out loud.

"They're trying to get it," said another, adding to the Rat King's thinking.

"We could help them get it," said a third.

Kit wondered if any of the voices speaking was Eeni's mom. Eeni was probably wondering the same thing.

"Can a berry be delicious?" the Rat King asked Eeni.

"Yes," said Eeni, crossing her arms and tapping her back paw impatiently.

"Can a berry be poison?" the Rat King then asked.

"Duh," said Eeni. She couldn't talk back to her mother directly, but she could talk back to whatever her mother had become. Kit knew that Eeni's sarcasm was her way of saying *I love you.* She was not a sentimental rodent.

"Can the same berry be delicious for one animal yet poison for another?" the Rat King said.

"Uh-huh," Eeni replied, unsure where the questions were leading. Her eyes scanned the bits of the Rat King she could see through the doorway, and Kit figured she was looking for her mom, but of course she would never recognize her mother. Rats in the Rat King all looked alike in time, and Eeni's mother had been a part of the Rat King for a very long time.

"So one berry can be more than one thing," said the Rat King. "Depending on who eats it?"

"Yeah." Eeni paused. "Depending."

"And so it is with all things," the Rat King said. "Food does not taste the same from one animal to another, nor do trees grow in the same soil. Not even rainbows touch the earth in the same places."

"See?" Eeni grumbled to the rest of the bakery. "Riddles again."

"You're talking about the zoo, aren't you?" Kit said the Rat King.

"Yes!" said one of the rats in the Rat King.

"He's got it!" said another.

"Sharp as a termite's tooth, that one is," said a third.

"We are indeed talking about the zoo," the Rat King said all together.

"But . . . uh . . ." Kit wrinkled his brow. "What are you trying to tell us about it?"

"To take care that you remember," said the Rat King. "Remember that what is a balm to some is a poison to another."

With that, the hundred-headed creature pulled away, and with a great scrabbling of claws, the heaving mass of black-and-gray-and-white fur disappeared into the night. The customers inside Possum Ansel's bakery stood dumbfounded.

"Well, *that*," Eeni declared, watching the doorway with tired eyes, "wasn't the least bit helpful."

"I made a hundred cabbage cakes!" Possum Ansel proclaimed as he burst from the kitchen with Otis the badger holding a towering tray of miniature cakes.

The possum's shoulders slumped when he saw the Rat King had gone. He'd been excited to share his cooking with someone so famous who also had a famously large appetite. He looked around at his usual customers and was crestfallen.

"I'll take a cake or two," said Blue Neck Ned. The Blacktail brothers stepped up to get their own as well. Everyone went right back to their old ways, scamming and scheming for a free meal, like nothing miraculous had just happened. That was the way of some creatures. They ignored whatever they didn't understand.

But Kit couldn't ignore it and neither could Eeni.

"What did that *mean*?" Kit asked his friend. "What's a *balm*?"

"Something for healing," said Eeni.

"So it's the opposite of poison," Kit said. "What could that have to do with the zoo? Is the zoo a poison or a balm?"

"Either? Both? Neither?" Eeni shrugged. "The Rat King

just likes to make things complicated. They don't actually say anything helpful."

"That's not true," said Kit. "They give us perspective."

"Pfft." Eeni waved her paws. "Some use *that* is. Doesn't change that we've got to break out our friends. Dax is in there and Uncle Rik and the others. Who cares about the Rat King's riddles?"

Kit noticed that Eeni hadn't mentioned his mother in her list. She was probably still thinking about her own mother and Kit thought it would be kinder to avoid the subject of mothers altogether for a little while. It wasn't like either of them could forget that they were rescuing *his* mother, while *hers* was still part of the giant tangle of riddling rats. *His* mother was trapped while *her* mother had chosen to leave her. This mission was, in a way, a balm to Kit but kind of a poison to Eeni, at least to her feelings.

But Eeni, like a true friend, was trying not to let her hurt feelings show. She was as committed to helping Kit as ever. Was that what the Rat King had wanted Kit to know? That feelings were complicated?

Like Eeni would say, *Duh!*

Or was it that creatures were complicated, that creatures were more than one thing, and maybe that a friend could be an enemy or an enemy a friend?

And that's when Kit started to form a plan.

He turned to Eeni. "Remind the rest of the Moonlight

Brigade to rest up, because tomorrow night we go back to the zoo!"

"You look like you just had one of your big ideas," she told him.

"I did," he said. "Before we get some rest ourselves, we've got to chat with an old . . . *friend*."

Eeni sighed. She saw Kit's eyes go through the bakery door across the alley to the windows of the People's houses and she knew exactly what "friend" Kit meant.

He wanted to talk to his worst enemy, the Flealess leader, Titus.

"I sure hope he doesn't try to kill you this time," she told Kit.

"I'm sure he'll try," Kit said with a shrug. "But he hasn't managed it yet."

"What if he gets lucky?" Eeni couldn't hide her worry.

"Don't worry, old pal of my paw," he reassured her. "I'm a raccoon. I make my own luck."

Part II

~~~~

THERE ARE NO ZOO ANIMALS

Chapter Nine

MISNOMERS

TITUS was a miniature greyhound, twice as vicious as he was small, and he was quite small indeed. His People spoiled him, which made him look down on any animal who wasn't equally spoiled, and most of all he looked down on the Wild Ones, who lived free in the alley behind his home. He'd tried to destroy them over and over but he had failed every time.

Titus blamed Kit for all his failures, so it was no surprise that he began barking the moment Kit scratched at the rear window of his house.

His People, however, were deep sleepers and didn't stir at his alarm.

"They've gotten used to your yapping," Kit said, loud enough for the dog to hear through the glass. "Maybe it's time you learned some new tricks. Although maybe you're too old to learn anything new."

"Go away, Kit," Titus snarled. "I've got nothing to say to you!"

"Come on, Titus," Kit taunted him. "You can do better than that. Or have you gotten soft in your old age?"

"Soft! Old!!" Titus snapped. "I'm tougher at nine than when I was a pup and I could tug your tail off if I wanted to!"

"Nine!" Kit scoffed. "I didn't think dogs could even get so old! Then again, you do look like a dog on his last legs . . ."

"How dare you insult me, you flea-filled sack of worm meat!" Titus replied.

"Well, you're a shampoo-stinking leash lover!" Kit taunted, which made Titus howl furiously, just like Kit wanted.

The lights in the house snapped on and a tired-looking Person stumbled to the door, muttering something. Kit hid himself as the door was cracked open to let Titus out.

Titus charged into the dark, barking, and the Person vanished back inside.

"Say that to my face, Kit!" Titus barked. "I'll turn your head into a chew toy!"

"Whoa, calm down." Kit held his paws up in surrender. "I don't want to fight. I just want to talk to you."

"Well, I don't care for talking," Titus growled, and lowered his head, preparing to pounce.

"I thought you'd say that," Kit told him, then whistled his signal to the rest of his gang.

At the sound, the young heroes of the Moonlight Brigade popped from behind trash cans and from on top of roofs, and even burst from burrow holes in the ground below. Eeni held a rusted fork as a spear, and Matteo the mouse aimed a flaming matchstick arrow from his rubber-band bow. Hazel the rabbit twirled a paper-clip chain and even Guster and Guster Two scowled fearsomely, or at least as fearsomely as moles could scowl.

Kit crossed his paws and tapped his foot, waiting for Titus to reconsider his attack.

The dog sat back. "Fine," he grumbled, seeing himself surrounded.

He should have known better than to chase Kit outside into the alley, which was Wild Ones turf. The dog had let his anger get the better of him. Dogs never could control their tempers, and that was why raccoons would always outsmart them. Kit knew that a thinking fellow would always beat a barking one.

"You know more about People than I do," Kit told him. The dog didn't disagree. "Tell me, what do you know about the zoo?"

Titus flinched. "The zoo? I don't know anything about the zoo! Why should I? The Flealess have been house pets for generations! My mother's mother's mother's mother was a house pet. And so was hers! We don't go anywhere near the zoo and we don't want to. It is not a place for our kind. We would never allow ourselves to be locked up for the People's amusement like that."

"But you're locked up for the People's amusement now!" Eeni observed.

"You know nothing of the Flealess!" Titus said. "The People live to serve us! They entertain us and do as we ask. When I want a treat, I tell them and they give it! I eat right from their hands and lick the smells right from their fingers when I want to. When I want a nap, I push them from their beds and I take a nap! They even pick up my poop for me and accompany me on my patrols of the neighborhood."

"On a leash," Eeni scoffed.

"Yes," said Titus. "That is so they go where I want them to."

"But they put the leash on you," Kit said.

"I allow them to put it on me," said Titus. "They seem to enjoy it so. And I am a generous dog."

"But they lock you up when they want to," Kit told him. "How is that any different from the zoo?"

"Because it is!" Titus barked. "Because I live in a real house with real things, not some painted cage like the zoo animals!"

"There's no such thing as a zoo animal," Eeni objected. "That's a misnomer."

"A miss-what?" Titus wrinkled his brow. Kit smirked. Eeni loved using her big words, and Kit loved it when someone else asked what they meant so he didn't have to.

"A misnomer," Eeni explained. "It means a wrong name. Like how fireflies aren't really flies, but beetles, though we call them fireflies anyway. And calling someone a zoo animal just because they live in a zoo is like calling you a leash lover just because you walk on a leash. It's insulting, right? There's more to you than leashes, right? Like, you're a tick-brained shampoo-stinking brat too, but you wouldn't want us to call you that to your face either."

Titus growled. Eeni could never let a chance to insult the dog pass her by, but Kit admired how well she explained things. No one wanted to be labeled by just one part of their life, especially when they had no control over that part. His mother wasn't a zoo animal. She was an animal who'd been trapped and put in a zoo. The zoo was what had happened to her, not who she was. And as soon as he broke her out, she'd never be called a *zoo animal* again.

"You lured me outside at this undogly hour of night to argue about words with me?" Titus said. "You are a very strange rat."

"Words make the world," Eeni replied. "And I thank you for your compliment. I'd rather be a strange rat than a mollycoddled dog."

"Mollycoddled?" Titus growled again. "I don't even want to know what that means. I'd rather sink my teeth into your neck than hear another one of your ridiculous words."

"Hey, enough of that." Kit pleaded for calm. "You don't need to get all defensive, Titus. I just need you to help me figure out what kind of lock they have on the animal cages at the zoo so I can pick one open."

"I couldn't possibly help you. I know nothing of locks," Titus said. "And I wouldn't help you even if I could. I have no interest in freeing a bunch of"—he looked at Eeni and grinned—"*zoo animals.*"

Eeni clenched her teeth, fighting the urge to spear Titus in the snout with her fork.

"I just need to know what this is," Kit said, and he used his claws to draw a picture in the dirt, the little box with the buttons on it that was next to the door to his mother's cage.

Titus cocked his head. *"That?"* he scoffed. "How

could *that* help you? That looks like the buttons on a telephone. People push the buttons in a certain order to talk to one another."

"So it's like a riddle," Kit said. "Pushing the buttons in the right order makes something happen?"

Titus grunted. He either didn't know or wasn't going to answer.

But he'd told Kit everything he needed to know.

Kit closed his eyes in thought, imagined how he might solve the riddle of the buttons to open the cage . . . He was starting to get an idea. "You lick their fingers, huh?" he said, grinning.

Titus was puzzled. "What's he talking about?"

Eeni shrugged. She didn't know either. "Kit?" she asked him. "You look cagier than a cowbird in a canary nest. You're up to something, huh?"

"I am," Kit said, then he turned to Titus. "Thanks for the help, old friend."

"We aren't friends!" Titus whined. "And I didn't help you at all!"

It was Kit's turn to shrug. "Let's go, Moonlight Brigade! Stand down!" Kit started to walk away, then stopped and turned back to the Flealess dog. "And Titus, watch your step. Wouldn't want you to get hurt out here in Ankle Snap Alley. It's no place for an old dog like yourself."

At that, Kit's friends lowered their weapons, and Kit turned his back on his enemy. Titus seized the opportunity . . . just like Kit knew he would.

Titus sprang at Kit's back, teeth bared and claws thrashing.

"Watch out!" Eeni shouted, but Kit didn't even flinch. He closed his eyes and listened for the loud *SNAP!* And then the *yelp* that followed.

Titus had sprung one of the People's mousetraps that all the wild animals knew better than to step on.

"Owee owee owee!" Titus whimpered and rolled on the ground. He'd caught the trap on his back toes. It wouldn't hurt the dog forever, but his paw would be sore for quite a while.

"I warned you," Kit said, and he and his brigade left the dog to crawl back to his door, whining for his People to let him back in.

The sun was just beginning to rise when they returned to the empty apartment in the big oak tree, and Kit yawned, but started pulling Uncle Rik's books from the shelves to help with the plan forming in his head. Kit liked the quiet magic of reading that could put a raccoon in a rabbit's shoes, or send him to the moon on a meadowlark's wings, or simply let him sit by the glow of a lightning bug and learn from his ancestors, who'd written their wisdom long before Kit was even a scent on the breeze.

"It's going to be a long night tonight," Eeni said, resting a paw across the first book Kit had pulled down: *Smellopedia: A Collection of Human Scents.* He wanted to study as many different people smells as he could before he returned to the zoo. "What we need to do is get some sleep."

"Sleep?" Kit couldn't believe his ears. "How can you want to sleep at a time like this?"

"I can want to sleep anytime," Eeni said. "A good thief knows that sleep's the only thing in the world you can't steal from. Sooner or later, it'll take back what it wants."

"But we need to get ready for the zoo break!" Kit argued.

"Sleeping is part of getting ready," Eeni replied. "You ever hear the story about Azban, the First Raccoon, and the Great Goose Heist?"

"No," Kit said. "I haven't heard that one."

"Because it never happened," said Eeni. "Azban planned all night, and was so tired that he slept right through the goose feast and never got to steal it. You won't be a lot of good to anyone if you stay up all day reading and fall asleep in the middle of the breakout tomorrow night."

Kit frowned at his friend, but she was right.

And she was also curled up on a mossy pillow, snoring quietly, by the time he put the book back on the shelf. He chuckled to himself and curled up on the leafy sofa, thinking about reuniting with his mother, and saving his uncle, and bringing all his friends home again, a hero. He was feeling impatient and wanted to pop up and run to the zoo and tear open the cages right away. He didn't like waiting. He didn't like how the quiet settled over him like a thick blanket or how the golden morning light made the window shade glow or how the giant raccoon in front of him seemed to float above the floor . . .

That was when Kit realized he'd already fallen asleep and was having a most peculiar dream.

Chapter Ten

THE ONCE AND FUTURE RACCOON

THE giant raccoon in his dream blinked and suddenly he and Kit were standing outside and it was night. The raccoon glowed like the sunlight coming through a window shade, and a twinkle like starlight lit his eyes. His eyes were, in fact, filled with shining stars.

The raccoon held up its front paws, touching the tips of its claws together to form the raccoon salute, an *A*, which was the symbol of Azban, the First Raccoon. Kit returned the salute and the raccoon—who Kit was pretty sure was Azban himself—beckoned for him to follow.

Kit—never one to argue with a mystical dream ancestor—stood and followed, glancing back once to the apartment where he was actually still sleeping across from Eeni. She was snoring slightly and muttering about pizza.

"Where are we going?" Kit asked, as he scurried to catch up to Azban. The dream raccoon drifted above the ground rather than walking on it.

Apparently, this was one of those dreams where Azban didn't speak, because he just pointed and Kit saw that they were still in Ankle Snap Alley, but it was Ankle Snap Alley from a long, long time ago, back when it was just fields and meadows, with a few ramshackle houses for People.

He and Azban stood outside one of those houses and they saw a raccoon on the porch, wearing a fine jacket and puffing on a long corncob pipe, sitting beside a Person, who was also puffing on a long corncob pipe.

"Is that you?" Kit asked.

Azban nodded beside him.

Azban on the porch spoke to the Person and, much to Kit's surprise, the Person spoke back.

Dreams are weird, Kit thought.

"Listen here, Cousin Farmer," Azban on the porch said between puffs of his pipe. "I think I'd like to set your dogs free. It's not right keeping folks as pets."

"My dogs like being pets," said the farmer. "And I like having 'em."

"The Person understands him?" Kit asked with surprise.

Dream Azban, floating beside him, touched a paw to his lips, telling Kit to hush, and Kit kept watching the farmer and the First Raccoon. This was a long time ago indeed, back when People and animals still talked to each other.

"Well, how about this," suggested Azban. "I'll bet you their freedom, against all the fur on my hide, from snout to tail, that I can pluck a star down from the sky and eat it."

"Oh no, Cousin Azban," the farmer said. "You've tricked me too many times. I won't make any more bets with you!"

"You can even pick which star," Azban said.

The farmer looked up at the sky, but inside the farmer's house a hunting dog growled.

Kit noticed Azban's back paw was curled, like he was hiding something from the farmer. The paw glowed, but the farmer didn't see it. He was looking at Azban's fur and thinking of making it into a hat.

"Don't take the bet," the dog shouted. "I *like* being a pet!"

The farmer ignored his dog's advice. "I'll take that bet," the farmer said, his greed getting the better of his good sense. "I want you to pluck that star there!"

The farmer had pointed to a bright star shining at the

edge of the horizon. Azban smiled and stuck out his empty paw. "Shake on that," he said, and the farmer shook his paw.

Then Azban bent down to set his pipe on the ground, "So it won't spill," he said. Kit saw him snatch the glowing thing from his back paw with the front paw the farmer had just shaken, but the farmer hadn't noticed.

"Fireflies!" Kit exclaimed. "He's got a firefly in his paw!"

Azban in his dream hushed him again. He watched as the raccoon on the porch stretched up on his back paws and reached high into the sky. With some sleight of paw, he slipped the firefly from his clenched fist to the tip of his claw.

"Look closely now," said Azban to the farmer. "I don't want you to think I cheated."

The farmer stared at the star he'd chosen.

With a little squeeze, the annoyed bug at the tip of Azban's black paw lit up brighter than the stars. Azban kept the firefly lit as he plucked it like a berry and popped it into his mouth. His cheeks glowed bright while the farmer watched, drop-jawed.

The farmer looked from Azban to the spot in the sky where the star had been. The problem was, he'd stared so hard at the glowing firefly, he had a blind spot in his eyes, as any folk who'd stared too long at the sun would know. Azban certainly knew that staring at bright light in the dark would blind a Person for a little while. The farmer couldn't see his star anymore, and had no idea that he'd had his eyes tricked.

"But . . . how did you—but?" The farmer was flabbergasted.

"You saw my paw was empty," Azban said. "You shook it. And then I took the star down and ate it, like I said I would. A bet's a bet. Gimme your dog."

"A bet's a bet," the farmer agreed, and stood, opening the door to his house.

In the doorway, the dog stood motionless, his tail tucked between his legs. He was, to use one of Eeni's favorite words, *nonplussed* . . . He was so shocked he couldn't speak!

"Go on, Duke," said the farmer. "You're free now to do as you please." Then Kit saw the farmer wink at his dog.

That brought the dog back to his senses. The fur on his back bristled and his eyes narrowed. And then he sprang at Azban, teeth bared to bite.

The dog barked curses at Azban and chased him from the porch. He ran as fast as he could up a tree, while the dog barked at him below.

"What are you doing?" Azban called down from the high branch. "I set you free!"

"I am free," the dog barked up at him. "I am free to eat you!"

The Person stood on his porch laughing and laughing. "I may get my raccoon-skin hat yet!"

"But . . . but . . ." It was Azban's turn to be nonplussed. The fast-talking raccoon couldn't find the words. Dream Azban standing beside Kit shook his head, embarrassed by himself.

"You can't give a dog freedom and expect him to run off on his home," the farmer said. "I give my dog food and a warm fire. What can you give him, Azban? What does the wild offer that's better than a dog's life at home?"

"Freedom!" Azban shouted down from the tree. "It offers freedom!"

"Your freedom's got you hiding up a tree." The dog laughed at Azban. "I'll take my spot by the fire any day." With that, the dog turned and trotted back up to the porch of his home. "Now leave us be, or I won't go so gentle on you next time."

The farmer and the dog glared once more at the raccoon in the tree, then slammed the door and left him outside, still high up in his tree.

"You won the bet, but still lost," said Kit. "The dog didn't want to be set free."

Azban nodded.

"You probably shouldn't have tried to bet for something the dog didn't want," Kit said.

Azban nodded again.

"Why are you showing me this?" Kit asked.

Azban turned and placed a paw on his shoulder. He looked squarely at Kit and the stars in his eyes glowed like fireflies. Kit's heart raced, eager for the wisdom that the First Raccoon would share with him. "Wake up," he said at last. "Wake up, you flea-bitten fur-brain!"

"What?" Kit gasped.

Azban jabbed a finger at Kit's nose. "Wake up!"

Kit opened his eyes and saw Eeni standing on his chest and poking him in the nose. "Wake up!" she repeated.

Kit yawned and looked around. He was on the leafy sofa in the apartment and the light through the shade had dimmed to nearly nothing. The sun had set and night was come and it was time for him to wake up. It was time for him to set his friends and family free. Whatever his dream had meant wasn't quite clear to him. The animals he was about to break out weren't house pets and they certainly wouldn't choose to be trapped in the zoo. Why had Azban shown him that story?

"I saw Azban," Kit said. "I saw Azban steal a star and free a dog and get chased up a tree as his thanks."

"I once had a dream where I lived inside a cabbage and was married to a talking nut," said Eeni. "If nuts could talk, how would we ever eat them?"

"Uh . . ." Kit didn't have an answer to that.

"Sometimes a talking nut is just a talking nut, and it

doesn't really mean anything," Eeni explained. "Point is, we've got some animals to rescue and no more time for dreaming."

"Let's get the Moonlight Brigade together," Kit agreed. "And let's get to the zoo."

Chapter Eleven

FALLING FOR FREEDOM

THE zoo was locked up tight for the night, which didn't mean much to a raccoon like Kit. With some quick climbing and a scurry or two, he found his way in over the fence. Eeni slipped in underneath it, and the rest of the brigade followed her.

"Keep your wits about you," Kit told them. "And don't get caught."

"What is it that we're supposed to do here?" Fergus the frog asked, looking around wide-eyed at the strange scenes in the animal enclosures. Of course, being a frog, he looked at everything wide-eyed.

"I need each of you to hide somewhere on the path from the building with the fake Ankle Snap Alley to the spot where we just came in," Kit explained. "When I set our friends and family free, you'll each direct them to the next animal along the path, until they're out. That way, they can escape undetected by going from one hiding spot to the next."

"Why do they need to hide once they're out?" Eeni asked. "We could all just run for it."

"The People might see us and sound an alarm," said Kit. "We don't know what they'll do to keep us trapped, so we need to be careful. Hopefully, the peacock will keep a watch out for us too."

"I bet he's asleep," said Eeni. "Peacocks aren't like us. They sleep all night. *Beauty sleep*, they call it. Although I never found a bunch of bright feathers beautiful to begin with. Pretentious. Show-offy. They think they're soooo cool, but they're just arrogant birdbrains if you ask me. I'll take a wisecracking rat over a pretty peacock any day."

"My dear child, that would hurt my feelings if I held rodents in any esteem whatsoever," Preston Q Bright-feather proclaimed, strutting into a streak of silver moonlight that made his turquoise-and-purple feathers seem to sparkle like the stars themselves. Kit felt a little breathless with the bird's beauty, but Eeni just frowned.

Rats and peacocks rarely got along, thanks to an ancient trick the one pulled on the other. Time had erased most of the details, but it had involved a pickle barrel, a fancy hat, and a very steep hill. Try as Kit might, he couldn't figure out what the trick had been or why rats and peacocks would still be so mad at each other about it all these generations later. The story'd been forgotten but the grudge remained.

One of the reasons that history was so full of wars, Kit figured, was that folk put their grudges right into their children's ears before their paws were big enough to scratch on their own or their wings wide enough to catch the wind. There wasn't any real reason a peacock and a rat had to dislike each other.

"Regardless of that little brute's manners, Kit, I am glad to see you once again," the Peacock said. "Since your last visit, I asked around about you. I had no idea I was speaking to a fellow with nearly as much nobility as myself." The peacock gave a respectful bow.

"Okay . . ." Kit wasn't sure how to react. He didn't think of himself as particularly noble, but if the peacock was in a helpful mood, Kit wasn't about to argue with him.

"Come along," said the peacock. "There is an air vent that will give you access to the cage you seek."

The peacock led Kit and Eeni to the building he had

shown them before, but instead of approaching the window, he led them to an air vent around the side. Kit's claws immediately went to work loosening it so he could slip inside.

When Eeni moved to follow him, he stopped her. "I need you to wait out here," he told his friend. "Make sure everybody is ready to go when we come out again."

"You sure you'll be okay in there on your own?" Eeni asked.

"I'll be fine," said Kit. "I've got just the idea to open up the door to that cage."

"You just come back safely," said Eeni. "I don't want to have to rescue you from the zoo too."

"I promise I'll come back," said Kit. "Howl to snap."

With that, he slipped into the vent and made his way toward his mother's cage.

The metal was hot to the touch and it scorched Kit's sensitive paws. He marveled that People built systems of metal tunnels like this and designed complicated ways of warming their buildings instead of just warming themselves with fur or feathers like sensible folks did.

The duct behind the vent cover was a maze that turned and twisted. Twice Kit hit a dead end and had to turn back and retrace his steps. He finally found his way to the air tunnel that went right over the Ankle Snap Alley exhibit.

He could smell it and his heart pounded fast in his chest. He was only moments away from freeing his friends, from showing Uncle Rik how clever he could be, and from hugging his mother again.

In his excitement, though, he put his foot down on a grate he hadn't seen and it swung open beneath him.

He fell, a long hard fall, straight down into the fake desert that was next to the Ankle Snap Alley exhibit.

He landed with a *thud* and lay stunned on the ground.

By the time he came back to his senses, he was staring up at the open vent so high above him that he had no hope of jumping to it. There was nothing he could climb to it either. The walls of the exhibit were smooth concrete, painted to look like desert sky, except for the one wall that was thick glass and looked out into the big room where People could stand and watch. There were a few boulders lying around and a small pool that had a hose sticking in at the bottom to keep it full of fresh water.

He was so close to his mother, just on the other side of the wall, and yet he had, in a way, never been farther. He couldn't think how he'd get to her.

There was no sound in the strange exhibit but the *hiss* and *hum* of the air from the high vent. Nothing real was ever as quiet as this. The world was supposed to be full of noise—insects hummed and buzzed, animals argued and laughed, birds sang and gossiped and even the ground grumbled and shifted below your paws.

But inside this fake desert nothing moved and nothing made any noise.

Not even the three mongooses who'd watched Kit fall and now, without warning, sprang on him.

Chapter Twelve

MONGOOSE LAW, MEAN AND RAW

MONGEESE?

Mongooses?

Kit had no idea what to call more than one mongoose. He just knew that these three were trouble.

"Git his arms!" the biggest one yelled, as the other two pinned Kit's front paws to his sides. The biggest one jumped on top of him with his long body, pressing Kit flat on his back. "Who are ya? Who sent ya?" the mongoose demanded.

"I'm . . . uh . . . Kit," Kit said. "Uh, I sent me, I guess? But it was an accident. I was trying to get next door."

"You hear that, Chamcha?" the big mongoose said. "Raccoon here says he sent himself! Raccoon says he's here by *accident.*"

"I hear it, Baas," said the Mongoose named Chamcha.

"You believe it?" Baas asked as his strong paws pressed harder on Kit's chest.

"Nah, Baas, I don't believe it," Chamcha answered.

"How about you?" Baas asked the third mongoose, who didn't say anything, just snarled. Then Baas turned back to Kit. "Looks like nobody here believes you, son of Azban. So why don't you tell us the truth? Who sent you? Was it that pretty bird, Preston? You working for him? He send you? He send you to keep us in line?"

"What? No!" Kit objected. "He's helping me, but I'm here because I want to set the folks in the next cage free."

Baas gasped. "Free?"

Kit nodded.

"You're setting folks free?" Baas asked.

"Yeah," said Kit. "My family's trapped right on the other side of that wall and I want to free them."

"Just them?" Chamcha asked. "Why not us? What's so special about them?"

"Well, I know them," Kit said. "I don't know you."

"So just because you don't know us, we don't get freed?" Baas growled.

"No, it's not that," said Kit. "I didn't know you *wanted* freedom. I'm just trying to get to the next cage. I don't know anything about you."

"You know we're in *this* cage," Chamcha said.

"Well, yeah . . . ," said Kit.

"Seems pretty selfish to help out only the folks you know," said Baas. "Seems like you fall into our cage and want us to help you out, you gotta convince us."

"Convince you?" Kit didn't know what to say.

"We'll help you out if you can convince us," said Chamcha.

"In rhyme," added Baas.

"Rhyme?" Now Kit was really confused.

"Mongoose Law," Baas explained. "Show us what tricks your tongue can do, and maybe we'll let go of your claws."

"But you better rhyme like your life depends on it," said Chamcha.

"Because it does," Baas added.

The third mongoose growled.

"Okay, well, gimme a second." Kit thought. Eeni was much more poetic than he was. "I don't know what to rhyme about."

"Insults usually work," said Chamcha. "Like this. Gimme a beat."

The third mongoose stopped growling and put his paws to his mouth, using his lips to create a beat.

Chamcha bopped his head to the beat and then showed Kit what he wanted:

> *You look like an overweight kitten,*
> *flea-bitten.*
> *Punched in the eyes,*
> *left in a trash can,*
> *eaten by flies.*

"Or you could also say," Baas added, tapping along with the beat himself:

> *Flies wouldn't eat him,*
> *His face looks all beat-in.*
> *The great raccoon come looking for help?*
> *More like a buffoon, half-witted whelp!*

"Ooh, nice burn, Baas!" Chamcha cheered, then tried a really fast rhyme:

> *I could turn a raccoon into a hat,*
> *make his brains splat,*
> *sell it to a cat.*
> *But what kind of cat wants a hat like that?*

The mongooses laughed. "Your turn, Kit," they said.

"Do Preston," Chamcha suggested.

"Yes," agreed Baas. "Cut the peacock down."

"Why do you guys dislike him so much?" Kit asked.

"We don't need a reason," Chamcha told Kit. "You just need to rhyme."

Mongooses, Kit realized, were not very nice creatures at all. They were, however, pretty clever with their rhymes and Kit needed their help to get out of their cage and get to his mother. He'd have to beat them at their own game and win their loyalty. He'd have to insult Preston Q Brightfeather in rhyme.

"Okay," Kit said. "Gimme a beat." The third mongoose started a new beat with his paws at his mouth. It took Kit a while to get his head bopping to the rhythm of it. Then he started:

> *You want me to insult a bird some more,*
> *make up rhymes like you've never heard before?*

Kit cleared his throat. Then he burst out with rhymes as fast as he could think of them:

> *Yeah, I can spit up thorny verses about that*
> > *feather-headed fool,*
> *but before I lose my cool,*
> *go foam-mouthed mad when I take you all to*
> > *school,*
> *I got some words to say about your mongoose*
> > *hospitality.*
> *You got the jump and threatened my mortality,*
> *met me with brutality,*

> *but if you don't climb off my chest I'll cause you*
> *a fatality.*

He followed his verse up with a growl, which made the point clear.

"All right, all right, you've got some talent," Baas said, leaning back off Kit's chest and telling the other two to let his arms go. "But don't try anything. You're still our prisoner and we can still tear you to shreds."

"And you still need to convince us to help you," added Chamcha.

Kit stretched and stood up to stare at the mongooses eye to eye:

> *Still want me going after that bright bird?*
> *A strutting peacock whose feathers are absurd?*
> *He thinks that he's the greatest;*
> *he's just fakin'.*
> *Pluck his feathers naked,*
> *he's a slab of bacon.*

"Ooo!" Chamcha jeered.

Kit was on a roll. He snapped out some new rhymes:

> *Don't "ooo" me, mongoose,*
> *I'm not here to make friends.*
> *I want outta this cage;*
> *you're a means to my ends.*
> *You folks better learn that I don't play nice,*

so lift me up to that vent;
don't think I'm gonna ask twice!

"Not bad." Baas smiled at him. "Not bad at all, Kit. Any raccoon who can rhyme like *that* deserves the help of the mongooses."

"You know, rhyming-insult battles are a terrible way to decide to help someone," Kit told them. And then he realized the mongoose had said his name. "Wait! You knew who I was this whole time?"

Baas grinned. "Everyone knows who you are, Kit, leader of the Moonlight Brigade. Word spread fast that you were here at the zoo. Why do you think we loosened the grate up there?" He held up a battered-looking fake rock and a paw full of bent screws. "We wanted to meet you, but we needed to know it was really you. I figured only a real son of Azban could rhyme like that without practice. It took Chamcha three nights to think up rhyming *kitten* with *flea-bitten.* But you rhymed *naked* and *bacon* on the spot!"

Kit felt himself puff a little with pride even though *naked* and *bacon* didn't actually rhyme that well.

"So you'll help us out if we help you out?" Baas continued.

"Yeah," said Kit. "I will."

Baas nodded at Chamcha and the other mongoose and

they scurried directly below the vent on the ceiling high overhead. Chamcha stood on his back paws and stretched his long body to its full height. The second, silent mongoose climbed up him like a tree trunk and stood on his head, stretching as high as he could. The two animals waved and wobbled, but stayed tall.

Kit stepped as far from the leaning tower of mongooses as he could, pressing his back up against the glass of their cage, then got a running start, scrabbling up their fur with the tips of his claws and trying not to injure them as he went.

"Ow!" said the first mongoose as Kit climbed him.

"Grr," growled the second mongoose as Kit climbed him.

"Eeek!" squeaked the last as Kit climbed him.

He planted his feet on top of Baas's little head, bent his knees, and launched himself at the ceiling. The three mongooses tottered and toppled in a heap of fur, but Kit caught the edge of the air vent with the tip of his claw. His legs dangled and he had to kick them to scramble back into the vent, but he made it.

Then he turned back and helped haul the mongooses one by one up into the vent.

"That was a lot harder than loosening the screws," Chamcha panted; he peered down from the opening. "It looks a lot higher up from this side."

"I know," said Kit. "I fell through it."

"Yeah, sorry about that." Baas shrugged. "Mongooses gotta mongoose."

Kit didn't know what that meant, but he left them to catch their breath while he made his way toward the vent over his mother's cage. Baas called out to him before he got there.

"There are a lot of folks in this zoo who want to get out," he said. "You'll help all of them?"

"Well, I . . ." Kit hesitated. He didn't have a plan to break everyone out, just his friends and family. But he couldn't very well leave all the other animals trapped in the zoo too. In his dream, Azban had tried to free a house pet who hated him. If Kit was really the brave raccoon he thought he was, he'd have to try to free all the animals, not just the ones he knew himself.

He'd have to change his plans.

He'd have to open all the doors in the zoo, not just the one that held his mother and his uncle and his friends. He couldn't do this quietly; all the animals running free at once would cause a ruckus that might get them caught. But even though freedom for everyone was worth the risk, there wasn't enough time for him to get to every cage. The night would end and the People would come back. He needed to break everyone out *before* the People came back. He didn't need only to open all the doors in the zoo, he needed to open all the doors in the zoo *at once*.

He sat back on his haunches and thought. He thought about the lock with the buttons and the symbols that were beside the exhibit doors, the strange riddle locks the People had built, and he looked down at his own little paws. He looked at the mongooses and their little claws and the little pink noses sniffing the air.

He had an idea.

"Who else has thumbs?" Kit asked.

Chamcha grinned.

> *He can't do it alone,*
> *he's just a little raccoon.*

Baas replied:

> *We've got to introduce him to our old friend,*
> *the mighty big baboon.*

Chapter Thirteen

OLD
FRIENDSSS

KIT and the mongooses followed the vents back outside into the cool night air. Before he left, Kit took a long glance at the tunnel and sighed.

"I promise I'm coming for you, Mom," he whispered to himself. "I just have to help a few other folks out too."

"Hey, Kit." Eeni came up to him, her head cocked to the side. "These three do not look like who you went in there for."

"These are some new friends of mine," Kit said. "There's been a change of plans."

"We're busting the place open!" Chamcha cheered.

"Kit, I am very displeased with this," Preston Q Brightfeather clucked. "I did not send you in there to make friends with these ruffians!"

"They aren't ruffians!" Kit objected. He wasn't sure what the word *ruffian* was supposed to mean, but it didn't sound nice at all.

"We actually are ruffians," Baas said.

"And proud of it!" Chamcha added. "Unlike this overdressed chicken." He laughed as he pointed at the peacock, who fluffed his feathers and looked down his beak at them all.

"Kit," said Preston. "I agreed to help you free your friends and family from this zoo. I did *not* agree to help cause a general outbreak and disruption to the entire place. That I cannot abide."

"You cannot *abide*?" Kit couldn't believe his ears.

"*Abide* means to accept or act in accordance with," Eeni explain.

"I know what it means," Kit said. "I just can't believe he's saying it!" Kit whirled on the peacock. "So you can *abide* that the People lock animals up in zoos, just not that they lock up animals you don't like. You can *abide* that some animals are stuck here who don't want to be?"

"We live a good life here in the zoo," Preston replied.

"All of us are fed and protected and cared for. It is a wonderful place and the People are generous and kind to us."

"But you're not free!" Kit said.

"We are safe!" Preston replied. "We are happy!"

"Speak for yourself, you flightless feather face," said Chamcha. "It's too bad your brain works as well as your wings."

"At least one of them's pretty," said Baas.

"Enough!" Kit put himself between the mongooses and the peacock before they started fighting with more than just sharp words. "We don't have to fight. No matter our different shapes and sizes, whether we sleep in beds or burrows, houses or holes, we're still All of One Paw, aren't we? No matter who we are or where we live, we can help one another out because it's the right thing to do. Or is it really an every-claw-for-itself kind of a world?"

The peacock looked down in thought, then finally looked up at Kit again. "I am sorry," he said. "I am a solitary bird and I am not used to cooperation. But you are right, I will help you."

"Thank you," said Kit.

"He changed his mind really fast," said Eeni, with doubt in her voice.

"Your friend makes a compelling argument, don't you think?" said Preston to her.

"I do . . . ," Eeni agreed, but her sentence trailed off. She looked doubtful, but Kit didn't want to offend the only help they had who knew his way around the zoo, so he gave Eeni a look that asked her to hold her tongue.

"Do you know where the monkey cage is?" Kit said. "I need to get the help of the baboons and their thumbs."

"Of course," said Preston. "Very good idea. I'll take you. It's just this way." But then, before moving, he stopped. "I will not, however, escort the mongooses. They have been very unkind to me and I would prefer not to spend a moment longer in their rude company."

"You want to see rude?" Baas started:

> Gimme a beat.
> You don't like a mongoose?
> So what? We don't like your birdbrain or your
>   bird strut.
> Say another word, and we'll kick you in the
>   bird b—

"Stop it!" Kit cut him off. "Baas, Chamcha, it'll be fine. If you guys just follow the path to that next lamppost, you'll find my rabbit friend Hazel. She'll start you on your way out. Just keep following my friends and they'll get you past the fence, okay? I can take care of the rest here. Preston's not always nice, but he's on our side, right, Preston?"

The bird frowned. "I will not dignify their insults by being offended," he said.

"Okay, good," said Kit. "Then, let's go. Show Eeni and me to the Monkey House."

"Right this way." Preston gestured with a colorful wing, and Kit and Eeni made their way along with him. The mongooses watched them go for a moment, then turned in the opposite direction toward the first member of the Moonlight Brigade. Kit felt good that he'd helped three animals escape the zoo, but they were not yet the three he'd come for.

However, with the help of the baboons, he'd be able to get everyone else out too. The sky was still a deep night black and the stars twinkled above, but hints of purple were creeping up at the horizon and soon they would turn pink with sunrise and then the blazing day would come. He couldn't waste any time.

They reach another squat brick building that looked a lot like the one his mother and Uncle Rik were being held in. There were drawings of frogs and lizards all over the front of it and Kit looked questioningly at Preston.

"The lizards are the People's idea of showing where the baboons live," Preston scoffed. "You know how People are. They rarely make sense."

That much Kit knew to be true.

Preston showed them yet another heating vent, although this one was sealed much better than the previous one, and Eeni had to squeeze first and help Kit get it open from the other side. It took a lot of shimmying and prying, and Kit could feel the time passing with every breath. He began to worry that he'd risked the chance of freeing his mother by agreeing to free the other animals too. If he didn't get the Urban Wild out tonight, he might not get another chance. When the People saw that the mongooses had escaped, would they lock down the rest of the zoo more carefully?

He had to hurry. By agreeing to do the right thing, he'd made his whole plan a lot harder.

They finally got the heating vent open, and Preston wished them luck. He did not intend to wait around for them.

"Do whatever you want," Eeni grumbled, and let the vent fall back into place between them. She and Kit then made their way inside.

"He can't help his attitude," Kit said of Preston. "He only knows how to be a peacock. He's not worldly like we are. He's probably never actually met real wild animals before."

"I don't trust him," Eeni said. "And also, why is it so *hot* in here?"

"These vents are supposed to be hot," Kit said, but this one felt even hotter than the one in the other building. By the time he plopped out of the heating vent into the dark corridors of the building, Kit was parched. Luckily, the

People had left a big yellow bucket in the corner filled with water.

He plodded over to it and took a sip, which he quickly had to spit out. It tasted like soap and mud. The mud flavor would have been nice on its own, but the People had gone and ruined it with soap. He made his way back to Eeni, disappointed and thirsty.

They looked around together and immediately saw that something was wrong.

There were no baboons. No monkeys of any kind.

The room was like an indoor courtyard with glass display cases all around the walls. The cases themselves looked empty. The floor below Kit and Eeni's claws was decorated with shadowy pictures of alligators and iguanas and snakes: all reptiles, just like on the outside of the building.

"This isn't the Monkey House," Kit said.

"I told you I didn't trust that peacock," said Eeni. "Let's get out of here."

"Yeah," Kit agreed. He didn't have any time to waste in the wrong building. If the reptiles wanted to be free, he'd have to come back to let them out *after* he got the baboons to help.

As Kit and Eeni turned to go, a familiar voice spoke from one of the glass cases.

"Don't leave ssso sssoon," it said.

Its sibilant hiss was muffled slightly by the glass of its cage. Kit and Eeni turned together to see a yellow-and-brown python coiled calmly on a big fake branch that jutted across the middle of his cage. The python stretched his long body down so his head almost touched the glass and his eyes narrowed. "Ssso niccce to sssee you again, little Kit."

"Basil," said Kit. "They caught you."

Basil grinned. "They sssaved me," the python said.

Basil had been the enforcer for the Rabid Rascals, the gang that had ruled Ankle Snap Alley before Kit came along. He was the only reason folks had been afraid to cross the Rascals, but he'd betrayed his own gang to the Flealess, and when his plan backfired, he'd fled the alley all alone.

"I wasss ssstuck in a sssewer pipe when People pried me out," Basil explained. "At firssst, I fought them, but they left me in here and did me no harm. Every few days they brought me"—he winked at Eeni—"fresh meat."

Eeni shuddered.

"So you've turned into their pet?" Kit said. "Just like you always wanted."

"I live in luxxxury," Basil said. "I eat and sssleep and never know cold or danger. I don't even need to work! I am the king of all I sssurvey!"

Kit and Eeni looked around the dark room. There

really wasn't much to survey and Basil was stuck in his cage. He was a prisoner who imagined himself a king.

"I know what you are up to here, Kit," Basil said. "I know they have your mother."

"Yeah," said Kit. "And what does it matter to you? I'm not going to break you out."

"You are not going to break anyone out, Kit," Basil hissed. "I won't let you ruin the good thing I have here. I'm happy. A lot of of usss are happy here. Do yoursssself a favor and leave before you causssse more trouble than you can count on all your clawsss combined."

"Is this a warning or a threat, Basil?" Kit said.

"Maybe it'sss both," the snake replied.

"I'm not going to stop trying to help just because you like life in your cage."

"Ssssss." Basil sighed. His body began to uncurl from its branch, coil after coil, length after length, vanishing up into parts of the cage Kit couldn't even see. "You know, Kit," Basil said. "The People don't make their cagesss quite so ssssecure as they think they do."

With a ripple of muscle, the snake lifted himself completely out of sight inside his cage. Kit rushed up to the glass and tried to see where the python had gone, but he couldn't tell. There was a water dish, and a fake rock below the fake branch. There were bits of old skin the snake had shed, and there was a fake painted sky along the back wall. All the way at the top, there was a metal grate that the people could open and close to drop in the victims of Basil's appetite. And Kit saw the last flash of Basil's tail sliding out of it past the broken latch.

"Um, Eeni," Kit said. "We've got to run! Basil's loose!"

Before their claws could clatter back across the floor to the vent they'd come in through, Basil dropped his big scaly body from the ceiling and landed in front of them.

"You should not have come here, Kit," said Basil. "Although I am glad you did. Revenge isss, after all, a dish bessst ssserved cold- . . . blooded!"

Chapter Fourteen

WARM-BLOODED

"HEY, we've got no problem with you." Kit held up his paws to show he didn't have a weapon. Eeni stood beside him, scowling to look so tough she didn't need a weapon. "You can stay at the zoo if you like. We'll just be on our way to the other animals. We don't want any trouble."

"But you've got trouble," said Basil. "All kindsss of trouble."

With that, Basil whistled, and beside him, dropping from the ceiling all around the room, came three other serpents.

"Welcome to the Hall of Reptilesss," Basil hissed. "We're glad to have you for dinner!"

"I didn't know snakes could whistle," Eeni whispered to Kit.

"Meet my new friendsss," Basil said. "Atrox, Naja, and Thom."

There was a diamondback rattlesnake with a cruel grin, a black-necked spitting cobra with a deep frown, and a garter snake whose eyes bulged from his head.

"Hi," said the big-eyed garter snake. "I'm Thom. I'm really looking forward to eating you."

Kit had gone cold with fright, but not because of the snakes. Sure, they were scary, but he had a deeper fear. All the snakes had slipped from their cages. The fact that they all could have escaped whenever they wanted, but hadn't done so, was what really scared Kit. They had chosen to stay in the zoo. The mongooses wanted freedom, but what if other animals had learned to love being held here in the zoo just like the snakes? What if they didn't all *want* to get rescued? What if *his mother* didn't want to get rescued?

Like the Rat King had said, *There are as many truths as teeth and it is the ones you do not see that bite. Beware.*

What if this was what the warning meant? What if the Rat King had meant that Kit, by trying to help animals who didn't want his help, was dooming himself? What if freedom was, to some of the animals in the zoo, like a poison berry?

"Ssso," said Basil, grinning all the way to his ear holes. "Which to eat firssst, the big one or the little one?"

"Let'sss do both at once," said Naja the black-necked spitting cobra, as she reared up high over them and flattened her neck into a crown of shining black scales.

Threats to life and limb made all Kit's deep questions about freedom run right out of his head and his survival instincts took over just in time.

Naja spat a burst of venom. Kit and Eeni dove to the side in opposite directions, and it splashed across the floor. Basil snapped for them, but his jaws slammed shut on air.

His tail, however, whipped around to encircle Eeni. Like all bullies, the python went for the smallest victim he could find. His mistake, of course, was assuming that because Eeni was small, she was weak.

She was not weak at all.

As the snake's body wrapped around her, squeezing tight to make her pass out before he ate her, she pulled out a satchel she carried. It was filled with rosebush thorns, and the moment Basil squeezed too tight, they dug into him.

"Yowee!" he cried, and Eeni crawled straight out of his choke hold, running down the length of his body toward Kit.

"Well, don't hang around all day!" she said. "Run!"

Together, they ran for the front door, but it was locked

tight and Eeni couldn't even squeeze through the space underneath it. Basil and his three friends slithered after them.

"To the vents!" Kit shouted, and they rushed back the way they'd come in.

Basil and his nest of snakes gave chase. They could slither faster than Kit and Eeni could run, and the air vents turned and twisted in a maze of clanging metal hall-ways that the snakes' long bodies navigated with ease.

"We're not going to outrun them in here, Kit!" Eeni called over her shoulder to him as she ran.

"Just keep going," he told her. "Trust me! I'm right be-hind you."

Rats were, typically, good at mazes, and Kit trusted Eeni to lead them far more than he trusted himself. She ran with her side pressed against one hot wall of the air vent, and turned left and left and left again.

"They went thisss way!" Naja's voice echoed through the shining corridors, and the snakes slithered around a turn behind them. Atrox the diamondback rattled after them, but her rattle sounded faint. Kit dared to look back and saw the snakes falling farther and farther behind.

"The vicious vipers can't keep up with me!" Eeni mar-veled. "I must be the fastest rat in the world!"

Kit was panting and even more thirsty than before, but he kept running and the snakes kept falling farther behind them. Eeni turned a corner, then doubled back in the other direction and Kit stumbled, following. They slipped down a side branch of the vent system and stopped to catch their breath.

"Which way . . . did they go . . . now?" Naja's voice wheezed around them in echoes.

"I want . . . to eat . . . them!" Thom whined. "Basssil, you promised . . . I'd be the first . . . garter snake . . . in history . . . to eat . . . raccoon!"

"And you will be," Basil said. "But firssst . . . let'sss ressst . . . here . . . jussst for a moment . . ."

The python's voice was far away indeed. None of the other snakes said a word and the rattler's rattle had gone silent too. Then they heard the echo of all four snakes snoring.

"Are they *asleep*?" Eeni scratched her head with her tail. "Who goes to sleep in the middle of a chase?"

"Folks who get tired when it gets too hot," said Kit. "Folks who are cold-blooded." Kit grinned.

Eeni thought a moment, then burst out laughing and gave Kit a hug. "Oh, you clever trickster, you!" she said.

Kit knew that snakes didn't make their own body warmth like warm-blooded rats and raccoons. Cold-blooded reptiles took on the temperature around them. When they got too cold or too hot, their bodies slowed down to conserve energy. Kit had known they'd never be able to keep up in the hot air vents. They'd slithered themselves right into a long nap.

"Let's go clobber them while they're snoozing!" Eeni said, balling up her tiny fists. She had no fondness for animals who ate mice and rats by the score.

"No." Kit stopped her. "They won't wake up for hours. We're safe. We don't need to hurt them."

"But they'd swallow us whole if we were in their position!" Eeni complained. "It's only fair."

"Just 'cause it's fair doesn't mean it's right," said Kit. "We can't go clobbering all our enemies when they can't fight back. That'd make us no better than the snakes."

Eeni frowned. "Your heart's as mushy as mold on a mushroom," she said. "But I guess you're right. Just don't tell anyone I let 'em go unclobbered. Between the snakes and that hawk, folks are gonna start to think I *want* to get eaten."

"No," said Kit. "Folks will know you're merciful. Maybe they'll sing songs about you one day: Eeni the Merciful, who looked death in the eye and baked it a pie."

Eeni rolled her eyes. "I don't bake and you really aren't great at making up sayings, Kit."

"I guess not," he said.

Eeni led him back outside again, and Kit looked at the sky. The blue-black night was definitely getting lighter. Night was slipping by with every heartbeat and he *still* didn't know his way to the Monkey House, where the baboons lived. And now he didn't have the peacock to guide him.

"I can't believe that peacock betrayed us," Kit grumbled.

"I can," said Eeni. "The only animal folk I trust are the ones from Ankle Snap Alley . . . and even them I don't trust more than a whisker's worth."

Kit gave a grunt. He liked trusting other animals. He didn't want to spend his whole life being suspicious of every creature he met. He and Eeni had totally different ideas about who was who and what was what in the world, but that was what made them such good friends. By seeing things differently, they each saw more than they would have on their own.

"Preston didn't care about helping us. He just wanted to get rid of the Urban Wild creatures. When you changed your plans, he changed his, and now we've got to find the monkeys on our own." Kit paused, then clarified. "All baboons are monkeys, but not all monkeys are baboons."

"Okay . . ." Eeni said, unsure why it mattered.

"They might be more likely to help us if we're respectful of who they are and how they see themselves," he explained.

"How do we know *they'll* want to help, whatever we call them?" Eeni asked.

"I'll have to convince them if they don't," said Kit.

"Because I need more animals with thumbs." Kit looked around at the fenced-in areas along the path through the zoo. It looked like everyone who might tell him where the baboons lived was asleep. "The zoo People don't keep a lot of us night animals around, do they?"

"Guess the People want animals who will be awake when they're here so they can watch them go about their business," Eeni figured. "Although I haven't seen one place where an animal *could* go about their actual business! There's no businesses of any kind! And not one creature is wearing a stitch of clothes! It's like everyone here's playing at being animal folk even though they actually *are* animal folk!"

"Well, we have to find one of them to ask," Kit said. "We don't have time to sniff out every cage in the zoo."

He marched right over to the nearest animal area, a fenced-in meadow where two giant birds with long legs were asleep with their heads tucked under their wings. Kit had never seen anything like these birds before, but he cleared his throat and tried to wake them up anyway.

"Ahem." He coughed.

They didn't wake up.

"Ahem." He tried again.

Still nothing.

"Hey feather faces! Wake up!" Eeni shouted, and the birds' long necks bolted upright, towering high with tiny little bald heads on top. Kit and Eeni jumped back with fright.

"Ack! Who's yelling?" one of the birds yelled.

"Ack! You are!" yelled the other, then ran to the far edge of the fenced-in field and buried his head in a hole.

The other bird swiveled her head around and looked down at Kit and Eeni. "Sorry about my brother," she said. "He's frightened of everything. It gives the rest of us ostriches a bad reputation. We ostriches are actually a very brave sort, but my brother'd be scared of a church mouse."

"Actually, ma'am, church mice can be quite terrifying," Kit said. "I've gone into battle with church mice and I wouldn't want to be on their bad side. I'd be likely to stick my head in a hole too."

The ostrich—for that is what the large bird was—laughed. "Very funny, lad," she said. She cocked her head and blinked the long lashes over her eyes. "You must be the famous Kit everyone is talking about. Leader of the Moonlight Brigade, is it?"

"Uh-huh," Kit said. "And this is my right-hand rat, Eeni."

"Oh, we know all about Eeni," said the Ostrich. "Smarter than a sheep sheared in summer, they say, but as sneaky as a wolf wearing wool."

Eeni smiled. She liked having a reputation, especially one that came with a clever saying.

"My name is Camille and my brother is Clement," the ostrich said. "And you're looking for the Monkey House?"

"Wow, how'd you know that?" Kit marveled.

"Nothing stays secret in the zoo for long," said Camille. "Gossip flies faster than . . . well . . . flies."

"So can you tell us where it is?" Kit said.

"We've been warned not to help you, Kit," said Camille. "Preston made it very clear that there would be trouble for all of us if we tried to break out with you. He told us the world is quite frightening outside of these zoo gates."

"But ostriches are brave, right?" said Eeni. "So you're not afraid?"

Camille smiled. "Indeed not." She raised a long leg and used it to point down the path. "The Monkey House is the third building on your left. Promise us that when you figure out how to open these gates you'll let us out too."

"WHAT? WHAT WAS THAT?" Clement shouted from inside his hole.

"I promise," said Kit. "Will your brother be okay to run free?"

"He'll be fine," said Camille. "He's scared, but he's fast. As for you . . . you should move fast too. The last I saw, Preston was plotting something terrible in case you escaped the snakes. And he had help."

"What was he plotting?" Eeni asked. "Who was helping him?"

"He was with a little gray—," Camille began, but then her head shot up high and she yelped. Faster than a lizard licks its lips, she turned and ran to the back of the meadow and shoved her head into a hole in the dirt.

"Dog." Preston finished her sentence for her from behind them. "A little gray dog," he said.

"Hello, children," said Titus, standing beside the peacock. "What an interesting place this zoo is. What an interesting place for you to die."

And then the peacock and the leader of the Flealess sprang their trap.

Chapter Fifteen

SPRINGING INTO ACTION

THEY literally sprang their trap at Kit and Eeni with a spring.

BOING!

Preston used his foot to pull back a heavy spring that was mounted on a broken roller skate and then he let the spring go, catapulting a flying copper disk at Kit, the kind of metal disk that People used for money.

The small coin flew so fast it nearly shaved off the whiskers on the side of Kit's face. It shot into the side of a trash can with a loud *clang*.

"Moonlight Brigade!" Eeni shouted, switching instantly

into her command-rat voice. "We need backup! Defensive formation!"

At her command, from all their hidey-holes along the path, the Moonlight Brigade appeared.

Fergus hopped from behind a tree, while Guster and Guster Two instantly burst from the dirt. Hazel hopped over Fergus's head and bounded across the path, taking cover behind a light post, and Matteo, the brave little mouse, didn't hesitate. He charged down the path at the bird and the dog.

"Matteo, no! Take cover!" Kit yelled, but the ferocity of a mouse couldn't be held back with shouting, as anyone who has ever shouted at a mouse knows.

Matteo gritted his teeth, squeaked out a barbaric squeak drawn from the depths of his tiny soul, and leaped at the peacock's long blue neck.

Preston hissed and spread his massive tail, opening the bright plumed feathers like a shield, and he spun, twirling the massive wall of color at the little airborne mouse and knocking him clear across the zoo.

Kit rushed from his spot to go after Matteo and help him, but he hadn't made it three paw lengths before he heard the terrible BOING of the catapult firing again.

Another copper disk sliced at him, and he was forced to dive back for cover behind the trash can, where Eeni had shielded herself as well.

The coin sparked on the pavement where Kit had just been standing and skipped like a stone across a lake.

"I have more than enough of these little disks to last till sunrise," Preston said, reloading the spring. "People cannot resist throwing them into every pool of water they see, and I pay the crows handsomely to collect them. I could put more holes in you than a dog has fleas."

"Watch it, feather face," Titus grumbled at the peacock. "I haven't got any fleas and you know it."

"Apologies, Titus," said the peacock. "Of course, I meant *other* dogs . . . not you. You are one of the good ones."

"Thank you," said Titus.

"What are you doing here?" Kit called out to the dog. "This has nothing to do with you!"

"That's where you're wrong, Kit," Titus replied. "The moment you started asking about the zoo, I knew it meant trouble. I knew if you broke the animals out of here, I'd have more and more Wild Ones invading my neighborhood every day. I couldn't bear the thought! I also know that a zoo is a dangerous place for vermin like you . . . so I slipped from my home and made my way here to offer my assistance in destroying you and your wretched family the moment you free them from the cage."

"Preston?" Kit said. "You mean you were going to turn us over to the Flealess all along?"

"Don't be so shocked, Kit," the peacock answered him. "My loyalty is to my own kind, not to yours."

"But we're All of One Paw!" Kit howled, which made Titus and the peacock laugh.

"No, Kit," said Titus. "Some animals are simply better than others. And it is our right to do as we please with the rest of you. Now, Preston." He turned to the bright bird. "Let's finish this. Kill them all so I can go home and get some sleep! This nighttime skulking around is exhausting and I want to be home before my People wake up."

"Of course, Titus," said Preston. "My pleasure."

BOING!

A disk flew into the tree where Fergus the frog was hiding, cutting the bark as easily as a claw cuts a cucumber.

BOING!

A disk whistled at the light post where Hazel hid, clanging against it so loudly it woke the sleeping ducks in the pond. It nearly cut off the tops of Hazel's ears too.

"Hey, Preston! Keep down the noise!" the mama duck quacked at him. "Some of us are trying to sleep."

"Pardon me for attacking our enemies and defending the zoo from bandits," Preston replied. "I'm sorry my defense of our territory is interrupting your slumber."

The duck grunted at the peacock, then went back to sleep, without so much as looking at Kit or his friends scattered about the zoo's walking path. Sweet as they looked, ducks cared only for ducks, Kit knew, and he wouldn't get any help from them.

Kit peered around the edge of the trash can, but had to pull his head back quickly at the sound of another BOING!

The metal disk sparked off the trash can above him, then rolled along the path, coming to rest in a pool of light below a lamppost, the image of a Person's head shining up. Kit touched the small wooden token in his pouch, the paws within paws. He was closer than ever to finding her and giving it back to her. His journey would not end like this. It could not end like this! He would not be stopped by some arrogant peacock who thought the whole world existed just for his comfort. Kit would take this pretty bird down!

"He's got us pinned in place," said Eeni. "We can't move unless we stop that spring from firing. With that spring gone, we can charge straight at him."

"I know," said Kit. "But how do we stop a spring from springing?" He thought about the springs on traps, the way they stretched and snapped shut when they were released, the way they held tension in their metal coils, and the way to break them by taking that tension out or reversing its direction. "I got it!" Kit smiled. "But I'm going to need a pinecone."

He looked to the lawn and saw it was strewn with

pinecones, although there was nothing but wide open space between the pinecones and the trash can. He couldn't run to get them without getting a copper coin between the eyes.

Eeni understood Kit's wordless look as only a true friend will, and understood the risk of what she was about to offer as only a true friend can. "I'll distract them," she offered. "You run for the pinecones."

"Eeni," Kit replied. "I can't use you as bait."

"You already did with the hawk," she said.

"But we had the hawk fooled before we even started," Kit said. "We'd planned and plotted for ages. This is different. This isn't planned. It's just dangerous."

"Haven't you heard?" Eeni flashed Kit a crooked grin. "I'm sneaky as a wolf wearing wool!"

Kit nodded, knowing he couldn't talk Eeni out of being heroic when she had heroism in her head. "Okay, but if you get your head cut off by a flying metal disk, I'm going to be really mad at you. Promise you'll keep your head."

"Howl to snap," his friend said to him.

"Howl to snap," he replied, and then they bolted from behind the trash can, heading in opposite directions.

BOING!

The first shot was aimed at Kit, but went wide. He ran in a zigzag pattern so that it would be harder for them to aim at him or guess where he was running.

BOING!

Preston shot at Eeni, kicking up sparks just in front of her paws, so she had to jump and roll out of the way.

"Aim for the raccoon, you painted pigeon!" Titus yelled at Preston. "Ignore the rat. She's a distraction!"

"You're a distraction!" Preston yelled, swinging his springed catapult back around to aim at Kit.

Kit hit the lawn and rolled, scooping up two pine-cones, one in each claw, then he changed directions and ran at Preston. "Eeni! To me!" he yelled.

Eeni changed directions and started running toward him. They were coming at the catapult from opposite sides, and Preston froze, not sure if he should turn and shoot at Eeni or take aim at Kit.

"Do something!" Titus yelled. "Fire!"

The dog kicked the bird in the shins, which made him release the spring and fire off another copper coin with a deadly BOING!

Kit ducked the shot without slowing his run, and at the same moment tossed his second pinecone to Eeni, who leaped to catch it in midair. "Whoever gets there first," Kit said, and Eeni knew what he wanted her to do. But she also knew whoever got there first would probably get shot at first and she wasn't about to let that be Kit. The whole zoo was counting on him.

She sped up her run and shouted every insult she could think of to get Preston's attention.

"I'm coming for you, you worm-necked, tick-brained, flightless feather duster! You People-pleasing pusillanimous pus picker! You cockroach-kissing cage cuddler!"

She'd gotten closer than Kit, and Preston spun the catapult around, aiming straight at her. She charged him with her pinecone held up like a shield, even though she knew one of those copper coins would cut through it and through her behind it without even slowing down. She hoped it wouldn't hurt to have her head sliced off, although she felt bad for failing to keep her promise to Kit. She squeezed her eyes shut as she ran straight at her doom.

"Watch out!" Titus yelled just as Preston released the spring.

BOING-CLANG! AHHH! EEEP!

Eeni opened her eyes, and saw the catapult flip and the coin fly backward at Preston's head, forcing him to duck and cover, and making Titus yelp as it grazed his tail. A pinecone was stuck right between the coils of the spring.

Kit panted beside the broken weapon. When they had turned to shoot at Eeni, he had dived with an arm extended and shoved the pinecone into the coils just as Preston let it go, so the tension of the spring was absorbed by the pinecone and the spring itself backfired, shooting its metal missile at the shooters themselves.

Before the shooters could regain their composure, the moles had popped from their holes, Hazel and Fergus had charged, and Kit extended his claws and snarled. "Outnumbered again, Titus!" he said.

The dog and the peacock looked from one Moonlight Brigadier to the next, then to each other.

"This isn't over," said Preston. "This is far from over."

Before Kit could come up with a witty reply, Titus and the peacock had turned and run off in the other direction.

"They won't wait long before attacking again," Kit told the others. "We need to visit as many of the animals in this zoo as we can and get them on our side. When the time comes, we're going to need as many friends as we can find."

"On it, boss!" Fergus said. "And sorry about getting captured."

"Don't worry about it," said Kit. "Just don't let it happen again."

"Howl to snap," said Fergus.

"Howl to snap," Kit answered.

Fergus and Hazel hopped off to recruit the less predatory animals in the zoo. "I think I saw a deer pen," said Hazel. "I don't think deer will try to kill us."

The mole brothers said they would go talk to the prairie dogs. "Us diggers stick together, ya know?" Guster told Kit before they burrowed back into the ground and made their way beneath the safety of the dirt.

"Let's go get the monkeys," said Kit. "And hope the baboons are feeling helpful."

"Are baboons known to be helpful?" Eeni asked.

Kit didn't have any idea. He'd never met a monkey before . . . but he was about to meet a whole troop of them.

Chapter Sixteen

PEOPLE SAY WE MONKEY AROUND

THE baboons were legendary, but they were not to be trusted.

Kit had read all about them in Uncle Rik's books. In the long-ago times, baboons first tricked the sun into shining, then tricked it into shining only on the baboons. The First People had to give baboons their tails just so they'd share the sunlight.

It was said that baboons once took a storm cloud for a ride around the world and accidentally invented the hurricane.

It was also said that baboons liked riddles, which meant they'd be able to help Kit solve the riddle of the locks on the zoo cages, but Kit would have to convince them to help him first. He approached their cage with the hardest riddle he could think of.

"The more you take of me, the more you leave behind," he said.

He didn't even say hello first. Baboons, he'd read, did not think much of politeness. They thought manners were a kind of trickery.

"What's that?" A little baboon, about the size of Kit, scurried from a boulder where he'd been keeping watch over the glass wall that kept the animal exhibit separate from the People's area. It ran from the floor to the ceiling, made of thick glass that went the whole length of the exhibit. The back of the exhibit was a massive rock face rising higher than Kit could see, as if the baboons lived in a deep canyon. Of course they could leap and climb, so Kit figured there were other security measures the People had taken to keep the baboons in. Behind the boulders, Kit saw doors to smaller cages where the People put the monkeys during bad weather.

Kit breathed a sigh of relief that the baboons were not locked up in those cages at night. He'd never have been able to break them out if they were.

"I said," Kit repeated, as loudly as he could so the

baboon could hear him through the glass. *"The more you take of me, the more you leave behind.* What am I?"

The young baboon scratched his chin and pursed his lips. Then he broke into a wide pink-faced smile, the brown tufts of hair on either side of his cheeks spreading wildly. His big red behind shook with excitement. "A riddle!" he screeched, and jumped. "A raccoon's brought us a riddle! Wake up, everyone! A riddle!"

"A RIDDLE! A RIDDLE," a chorus of baboon voices screeched. From every rock and nook and cavern and cranny of the baboon exhibit, the big monkeys came running, a troop of a dozen males and females, all shouting with ferocious, fang-toothed glee.

Kit was, for just a moment, grateful for the wall of glass between them.

"Wow," said Eeni. "They really do like riddles."

"Repeat your riddle, raccoon!" a thunderous voice commanded, as the biggest male of the troop pushed his way to the front of the crowd, right up to the glass. He bent his head down so his eyes were level with Kit's and his breath fogged the spot between them. "I am Major Babi," he said. "And I will solve your riddle."

The baboon leader looked like no animal Kit had ever seen before. He was shaped something like a Person and something like a dog. His face was pink and free of fur and his forehead bald, but his cheeks and neck were ringed with a great tuft of white hair that gave him the look of a creature with wisdom. His long fangs and strong arms showed that with his wisdom came power.

His muscular arms were also coated in long gray fur that looked like a warm cloak, while in truth he wore no clothes at all. It was almost like People thought animals didn't deserve fashion just because they had fur!

The big naked baboon whipped his gray tail to the side and sat back on his spindly hind legs, resting his paws on his knees. All the other baboons, whose fur was neither so fluffy nor so grand as their leader's, looked to him.

"Speak," Major Babi commanded Kit, and all the baboons looked back at Kit, waiting. Kit knew that he was safe on this side of the glass, but still he shuddered.

"*The more you take of me, the more you leave behind.* What am I?" Kit said.

The baboon's long fingers scratched his chin. "Hmmmm," his voice rumbled.

"Hmmmm," all the other baboons echoed him.

"Ummmmm," his voice grumbled, and "Ummmm," all the other baboons replied.

"Ahh haaaa!" his voice shrieked, and he raised a single long finger into the air. All the other baboons burst into shrieks and applause.

"Did you get it?" Kit asked.

"I got it!" the baboon leader declared. "Are you a banana?"

The other baboons laughed and cheered, but Kit and Eeni frowned. From the corner of her mouth, Eeni whispered to Kit. "That's not it, is it? That makes no sense."

"No, that's not it," said Kit. "But look how happy he is . . ."

The baboon troop leader had stood on all fours and was hopping up and down, dancing and wiggling his bright red behind.

"I thought they were supposed to be the cleverest of all the animals?" Eeni shook her head, still whispering to Kit while they watched the baboon dance party on the other side of the glass. "Bananas? Your riddle is obviously not about bananas. The answer, if they even thought about it for a second, is footprints—"

Suddenly, all the dancing and shouting stopped and the baboons froze in place. Major Babi leaped with one powerful thrust of his legs directly in front of Kit again and pressed both his palms against the glass, baring his fangs in a wide, silent scream. Kit fell back startled, tripped on some kind of bench, and toppled end over end so his tail stuck up toward the ceiling. Eeni grimaced.

"Are you telling me," the large baboon snarled, "that the answer is *footprints*?"

"Well, sir, uh . . ." Kit stumbled back onto his paws. "There are a lot of ways to answer a riddle, I guess, and bananas are the kind of thing you leave part of behind when you eat them, but . . . uh . . . yeah . . . the right answer is *footprints*."

The baboon stared at him with fierce, heavy-lidded eyes and snorted hot air through his nostrils. Kit swallowed, part of him worried the baboon was going to smash through the glass right then and tear Kit's arms off for correcting him.

But instead, the baboon started laughing. *All* the baboons started laughing.

"I think the monkeys had their brains eaten," Eeni said. "Because they're all crazy."

"Baboons," Kit whispered back at her.

"Crazy Monkeys! More like Brilliant Baboons! Ha-ha-ha-ha!" Major Babi cackled, slapping his knees and rolling on the ground. "We're not the ones who just *told* us the answer to the riddle! Ha! And I thought the raccoon was supposed to be some kind of great trickster! Ha-ha-ha-ha! You just told us what the answer was and we didn't even have to rip your arms off! Some riddler you are!"

At that, the baboons redoubled their laughter. Something about ripping Kit's arms off seemed terribly funny to them. Kit and Eeni could do nothing but stand and wait for the fit of baboon boisterousness to end.

"Hey, what's three plus five?" Major Babi shouted through his gasps and cackles.

"Uh . . . eight?" Kit said, and the baboons screamed.

"He did it again!" one shouted.

"Ha-ha-ha-ha!" they roared.

"Oh, Kit!" Major Babi stood and wiped the laughing tears from his eyes. "A real trickster never answers a question. Why, we baboons haven't answered a question in over thirteen generations. And do you know why?"

"Uh." Kit thought about it. "No."

"HA!" Major Babi fell back into the crowd of monkeys as a whole new round of cackling commenced.

"You answered his question," Eeni said to Kit. "We'll never get anywhere if we keep answering his questions!"

"What should I do?" Kit asked her.

"Ask some of your own questions," Eeni suggested.

"Hey, Major Babi!" Kit called out. "How do you know my name?"

The baboon leader cocked his head and grinned. "How does anyone know anything?"

"Are you only going to answer my questions with other questions?" Kit tried.

"Who can see the future?" The baboon shrugged, but the twinkle in his eyes told Kit he was loving this. A chat with baboons was a game. He'd have to figure out the rules as he played, but it seemed that the goal was to keep the conversation going with only questions.

Maybe, Kit thought, if he could win, the baboons would help him. Or they'd try to rip his arms off. It was hard to know what these strange creatures would do, but Kit liked to assume the best about folks he didn't know . . . until they proved him wrong and tried to rip his arms off. He always wanted to be nice to everyone but he kept his claws ready just in case. "Do you know why I'm here?" he asked.

"Did your parents not explain that to you when you were younger?" the baboon replied.

"Have you met either of my parents?" Kit volleyed back.

"Should a monkey ask every raccoon he meets about her children?" the baboon said.

Kit's heart raced. The baboon had basically just admitted he knew Kit's mom! And he'd called himself a monkey, so maybe he wasn't all that interested in what Kit called him, as long as he played his games. He had to keep going. "Doesn't a baboon get curious?"

"Has a raccoon never heard what happened to the curious cat?"

"Is the monkey major comparing himself to a curious cat?" Kit noticed a few of the other baboons giggle at that one. Even Major Babi seemed to fight a fit of laughing, before he was able to get out his next question.

"Isn't a cat just an alligator snack?" he asked, and the other monkeys gasped. Kit shivered. The baboons had heard his story, how in the battle against the Flealess, Kit and Eeni had fed the cat-assassin, Sixclaw, to an alligator. These baboons knew exactly who he was, which meant they probably knew exactly why he was at the zoo. He'd had enough silly games. He wanted these baboons to help him. He had to win this game right away.

"Aren't all our enemies just a snack?" Kit replied coldly.

"Why should a baboon have enemies?" Major Babi said, grooming a bug from his shoulder and popping it into his mouth.

"Has a baboon never been in a fight?" Kit said.

"Isn't the clever one the one who never has to fight?" the baboon replied.

"Wouldn't the clever one be the one who is free to leave?" Kit said. "Like me." Then, without waiting for Major Babi to reply with a question of his own, he turned his back on the baboons and loped away from the exhibit. Eeni had to run to catch up.

"Kit?" she asked. "What are you doing? Don't you need their help for the breakout?"

"Just keep going," Kit whispered. "Don't look back."

"But what if they—" she started, when a loud BOOM BOOM BOOM interrupted her. She and Kit froze, then they slowly turned back to the glass exhibit window. Major Babi stood on his hind legs, his full height towering over the other baboons, and with two balled fists he pounded on the thick window so hard that it rattled in its frame.

BOOM BOOM BOOM. He pounded again.

Kit didn't move toward him, nor did he run away. He stood on his back legs, stretching up to his full height, which was dwarfed by the massive moonlit shadow of the baboon. Then he brought his paws together to form the letter *A*, the symbol of Azban, the First Raccoon.

Major Babi narrowed his eyes and then he touched the tips of his fingers together in the same gesture and bowed his head.

All the baboons did the same.

"What just happened?" Eeni asked from the side of her mouth.

"I think I just won," Kit replied from the side of his mouth.

"What now?" she asked him.

Kit smirked, then dropped down on all four paws and walked back to the baboon cage. "Now we get these baboons to help us solve the riddle of the locks. And once they do, we get to work opening every single cage we can."

Chapter Seventeen

A CHEESY PROBLEM

KIT stood by a door in the wall next to the glass, a door that was almost invisible to the eye, but that he could feel by running his paws along its edges. There was a small panel beside it also set into the wall, but Eeni, standing on his shoulders, could reach it. She pressed on it and it swung open to reveal a box with buttons on it, just like the ones outside the other cages in the other buildings.

"Just like I thought," Kit said. "This is how they made all the locks. You have to press the buttons in the right order to open the door. They're like riddles."

"RIDDLES!" the baboons on the other side of the glass cheered.

Eeni studied the little box up close, staring at the odd shapes written on each button. "I could just chew through this!" she announced, opening her mouth to bite the soft plastic.

"NO!" Kit wobbled and nearly sent both of them toppling to the floor. "If you break it, the door will never open. We have to solve the riddle to open it, not smash the riddle-box."

"These zoo People are sneaky," Eeni said.

"Maybe there's no such thing as zoo People either," Kit suggested. "Just People who work at the zoo. But they do other People things too. *That's* how we're going to solve this riddle."

"It is?" Major Babi asked.

"Don't you trust me yet?" Kit replied with a question of his own, then stepped back toward the lock so Eeni could get close. "Eeni, I need you to sniff each button."

"Why?" she asked.

"Because the People eat things and touch things and the smells from those things end up on their fingers. The same fingers—"

"That they use to press the buttons!" Eeni finished his sentence.

"Exactly!" Kit said. "If we can tell which buttons they press, then we can press them too and open the lock."

"Got it!" Eeni started sniffing, her little pink nose

working its way over each button. "This one smells like plastic. This one too. Ooh, this one smells like pickles and mustard. This one like mustard and cheese. This one has a chemically smell, but it's chemicals resting like a blanket over top of the pickles and mustard and cheese. This one too, although there's maybe some lettuce, and this one's got Swiss cheese. A lot of cheese. The rest just smell like plastic."

"So they press five buttons," Kit said. "Press the five with the smell of People food!"

Eeni pushed on the buttons but her little rat arms weren't strong enough. Kit stood on his tippy toes while Eeni sniffed and pointed him toward which buttons to press. His other paw tried to open the door.

Nothing happened.

Kit leaned on the door. It didn't move.

"Try again," Eeni suggested.

Kit tried again.

Still nothing.

"Are you pressing them in the right order?" Major Babi asked.

"Oh!" Kit remembered what Titus had said about the telephone. *People push the buttons in a certain order* to make it do what they want. These buttons were just like those, so they probably had to be pressed in the right order. But what order was that?

Eeni told Kit a different order to push the buttons.

Still nothing.

"Did you try them all yet?" Major Babi asked.

"Did he try them all yet?" Eeni scoffed. "Do you know how many combinations there could be?"

The baboons looked at one another and started counting on their fingers. "Is it five?" Major Babi asked.

"There are five different symbols on here that smell like they've been touched by people fingers," Eeni said. "So if each button gets pushed only one time, then there are five possible choices for the first one, then four for the second, and five for the third and four for the fourth, and three for the fifth. That's five times five times four times three . . ." She thought for a moment. "That's one hundred and twenty possible combinations! And that's *if* the symbols don't get pressed more than once!"

Kit was impressed by how fast Eeni was at math, but he was dismayed by how impossible solving the order was going to be. It was closer to dawn than to midnight, and they didn't have the time to try a hundred and twenty different answers to this lock, and then a hundred and twenty on the next one and so on. They'd never get any of the doors open that way.

"Which one smells the least fresh?" he asked Eeni.

Eeni sniffed. "This one, with the chemicals."

"Then maybe that one was pressed the longest time ago," Kit said. "So it would be first."

He pressed it.

"And the next weakest smell?" Kit asked.

Eeni sniffed some more. "This one's got more pickle in it and some of the cheese. Smells like a good cheese too," she said, and Kit pressed it. The next one was pickles and mustard but pungent, and then the symbol right in the middle had pickles and mustard, cheese, and just a hint of bologna, and the last was the most intensely cheesy. He pressed that last.

There was a *click*. Kit pushed on the door into the monkey exhibit . . . and it opened!

The monkeys cheered.

Eeni cheered.

Kit raised a paw to hush them all as he stepped inside.

"Listen, friends, we don't have time for speeches and I'm not so good at them anyway, but hear this: Tonight, you have been freed by the Moonlight Brigade. Freedom is the gift I give you, but I ask something in return. Will you pay this gift of freedom forward? Will you help me open the other cages so that any animal who wants to run free can do it?"

Major Babi approached Kit and towered over him, his mighty arms crossed in front of him and his heavy brow turned down. "You are asking if we will stay in this zoo, and risk the freedom we have just been given, to help others be free? Is *that* your question, little raccoon?"

Kit nodded.

"That is a stupid question," the big baboon said. "What kind of monkeys do you think we are?"

Then he burst out laughing and Kit knew the baboons were on his side. "The other Moonlight Brigadiers will help you with the smelling, but we'll need your height and strength to reach all the riddle-boxes. If you move fast, we'll have every door open by sunrise. But watch out for the peacock! He'll do anything he can to stop us."

Major Babi patted Kit on the head. "Why would a free baboon fear Preston Q Brightfeather?" he said. "Why would a free baboon fear anything at all?"

And with that, he howled a mighty howl and led his entire troop of monkeys past Kit and into their first night of freedom in the zoo.

"We just started a revolution, I think," said Eeni. "The People are not going to be happy about it."

"Well, let's make sure we're gone by the time they get here," said Kit. "You think you can sniff your way through some more locks?"

"Never doubt the scent of cheese," said Eeni. "There isn't a problem in the world that a rodent can't solve if it smells like cheese."

Part III

GOING WILD

Chapter Eighteen

THE BURDENS
BEARS BEAR

THE troop of baboons assembled with the rest of the Moonlight Brigade, who gave their reports.

"There are four deer on our side, ready to run!" Matteo the church mouse reported. He had a big cut over his left eye, which he'd bandaged with some sort of colorful sticker he'd found in a garbage can. It showed a baboon in a top hat. In their imaginations, People saw the animals more clearly than they did in their zoo.

"What happened to your eye?" Kit asked Matteo.

"A disagreement with a den of dingoes," said the mouse. Kit cocked his head, and the mouse explained. "At first, they thought I was their dinner. We had a bit of a . . . discussion about that." The mouse cracked his knuckles. "But once I showed them I'd be a better friend than snack, they came around. All of them are ready to join us."

"Great," said Kit. "Go with these two baboons and start sniffing out the locks. They'll explain on the way."

Matteo scurried into the palm of one of the baboons, and they ran off to start on the deer and dingo cages.

"No luck with the iguana," said Fergus the frog. "Or any of the other reptiles. Even the tree frogs in the tree frog case. I tried to explain they weren't even on real trees, but they wouldn't listen. Half of them just plain love their cages, and the other half are too afraid of the snakes and the peacock."

"We talked to the groundhogs," said Guster. "They weren't happy to be woken up, but they're ready to run free when we give the signal."

"The fish, however, could not be reasoned with," said Guster Two. "They couldn't hear us in their strange floating river, so we performed a dance to explain it. They did not understand. They just kept swimming in circles."

"I don't think fish can escape the water," Eeni said.

"We don't know what anyone is capable of unless we give them a chance," said Guster.

"So we had to ask," said Guster Two.

"But you're right," added Guster. "Freedom for a fish is totally different. I think we'll just leave them be."

"Okay," said Kit, and he sent Guster and Guster Two off with another pair of baboons to start work on the groundhog cages.

Hazel went with Major Babi and another baboon to open the Ostrich Meadow and a place called the Barnyard, where a bunch of goats and sheep and a sleeping cow were waiting to do whatever it was Hazel told them to do.

The rest of the baboons deployed throughout the zoo, hooting and hollering and banging on riddle-boxes like mad, while Fergus hopped to and fro after them, trying to slow them down and get them to sniff the buttons. A frog didn't have much of a sense of smell, but he could lick a button and learn a lot. He just had to get the baboons to hold him up to do it.

It was slow going, but Kit was satisfied that the work had begun. The sky was just beginning to turn pink in the far distance. Morning was still some time away, but it was coming. He and Eeni had to get back to the building where their neighbors, Uncle Rik, and his mother were held.

As they charged up the path, however, a bloodcurdling roar stopped them in their tracks.

There in front of them, blocking their way, stood the largest creature Kit had ever seen: a giant snow-white bear whose head was bigger than Kit's entire body, and whose paws could crush ten Eenis beneath them at one time if it wanted to.

"A *bear*?" said Eeni. "Preston sent a bear after us?"

"My name is Jojo," the big bear introduced himself, which was a good sign. Usually folks who meant to eat you did not introduce themselves first. "And yes, I am a bear. A *polar* bear to be precise. However, Preston did not send me. I came to meet you on my own."

"Oh . . . well . . . hi." Kit tried not to tremble at the sight of the giant white polar bear with teeth as big as Kit's arms.

"I wanted to meet you so that I could convince you not to do what you are doing," said the bear. "Not to break the animals from the zoo."

Kit's eyes darted around, looking for the dog or the peacock.

"They are not here," said Jojo, like he knew what Kit was thinking. "I am Jojo Walrus-Bane and I swear upon the honor of bearkind that I am not going to harm you by tooth or by claw."

"Okay . . . ," said Kit. "But you are going to stop us?"

"I am going to try to *convince* you," said Jojo. "The peacock wants to stop your breakout so that he can continue to have all the comforts the People give him. He is greedy. I promise you that I am not. I do, however, ask the same of you that he wants: I want you to turn back and to leave the zoo as it is."

"But why?" Kit asked, staring up at the humongous bear. "You're out of your cage already. Why wouldn't you want to give that freedom to all the animals?"

"I will return to my enclosure," said the bear. "I must. What you do not know, young raccoon, is that my kind are in danger. Our great northern wilds are shrinking away and year by year we polar bears are disappearing. We must hunt longer and harder for food. Our children starve; our fathers make war on one another. Families crumble like melting glaciers. The wild is failing us, but here . . . in this zoo . . . the People *protect* us. In places like this all over our world, they are restoring our numbers, keeping bearkind alive and safe."

"But you're a prisoner," Kit said. "You'd choose safety over freedom?"

The bear nodded. "My freedom would cost my brothers and sisters dearly. The People protect us but they do not see us for who we are. They do not know my name is Jojo Walrus-Bane, nor that my grandmother was Rustalka the Mighty, the great-general of the ice sea, whose life is celebrated in bear music around the world. To the People, I am just another frightening bear. If I am not in danger and in need of protection, then I am a threat in need of destruction. If I flee from the People's care, then every other polar bear will suffer. The People fear our freedom and will turn against us if we threaten them. So I stay. I stay to protect my kind . . . to show the People how to nurture us instead of hunting us. I stay to teach them."

"You shouldn't have to teach the People anything," Eeni objected. "It's not your job."

"But if I do not, who will?" said the bear. "And you, Kit, should be wary as well. They do not know you are Kit, heir to Azban the First Raccoon, and hero of Ankle Snap Alley. To the People, you are a trash-eater and they do not mean that as praise. They imagine you have Foaming Mouth Fever. Your crimes against them will be punished on the backs of all raccoonkind. Raccoons you have never met or known or shared a feast with will suffer when the People take their vengeance for your actions tonight."

"You make the People sound like monsters," Kit said.

"They are not monsters," said the bear. "They simply try to protect their own, just as we all do. But they have a ferocity that no animal folk can match. If you choose to carry out your escape, I fear the People will close this zoo. Many bears will suffer."

"But many animals *are* suffering in here already," Kit said. "You're asking me to let them stay prisoners to keep your kind safe. Aren't we All of One Paw?"

"I burn with shame from the tip of my nose to the claws

on my toes," said Jojo. "But I must think of my own kind first. There is a reason we say *to bear a burden* and not *to peacock a burden*. We bears do what we must and I must bear this burden for all bears."

"I understand," Kit told Jojo. "But my family and my friends and neighbors are being held here against their will and I have to free them. Anyone who's a prisoner is my kind, and that's who I'm setting free. If you change your mind, I see you know how to escape your cage on your own. You'll always be welcome to join us in Ankle Snap Alley."

"That does not sound like a good place for a bear," said Jojo.

"It's not a good place for anyone," said Eeni. "But it's home."

"Be careful, little ones." Jojo smiled sadly. "The fight for freedom can be a ferocious fight indeed."

"Hey," said Eeni, jabbing her tiny paw up at the giant bear. "You haven't seen how ferocious *we* can get. We're the Moonlight Brigade. We can teach them too. We can teach them that animal folk can't be pushed around. I'm not afraid of some no-fur two-leggers."

The bear nodded, then raised his paw to Kit and Eeni and clenched his massive fist. He pounded it three times on his chest like a drum. The bear salute.

Kit and Eeni returned the salute.

Jojo trudged sadly away into the night to climb back into his enclosure.

Kit marveled at his courage. If the bear wanted to, he could have smashed his way out of the zoo and torn the People who kept him there limb from limb. He could have been free any time he wanted, but he stayed a prisoner in order to protect other bears, bears that he'd never even met. It took bravery to run into a fight, but perhaps it took just as much bravery to avoid one.

Kit wasn't looking for a fight, though. He was looking for his family, and if he had to, he would fight to free them.

Chapter Nineteen

RIVERS
ROLL ON

KIT wanted to go alone into the exhibit hall where his mother was being held. He'd insisted in that stubborn raccoon way, but Eeni was not going to let her best friend just wander into a strange building by himself.

"I should come in with you," she said. "I have a better sense of smell."

"I'll be fine," Kit told her. "You just keep a lookout for Preston and Titus."

Kit knew Eeni didn't understand why he would want to go in alone, and he wasn't sure how he could explain it to her. It had been so long since they'd seen each other, what if his mother didn't recognize him? Or what if she'd heard about all the things he'd done—the tricks he'd pulled and the battles he'd fought—and what if she didn't approve? Or what if she was angry that he'd failed to rescue her sooner? Or what if, even worse, she'd become like Preston and the snakes and didn't want to leave the zoo at all? What if she would choose her life in a cage over him?

Fear kept him from speaking these worries aloud to Eeni, though. Sometimes a worry was like a spiky caterpillar and when spoken aloud it broke from its cocoon to fly away like a butterfly, but there were other times and other worries that hung on the tongue like stones. Kit wasn't strong enough to lift his worry into words and he didn't know that a friend can help with the lifting, so he said nothing.

"I'll wait right out here for you," Eeni told Kit at the vent they used to get in. "I'll make sure nobody gets past."

When Kit's paws found the vent opening, he flattened his body and slipped inside. Before he vanished completely, he called back to Eeni from inside the vent, with just his behind and his tail sticking out.

"If you're in danger before I come out and you need to run," he said, "you can run. I won't be mad. I don't know how long it's gonna take in here."

Eeni could tell Kit was stalling.

Of course he didn't know how long it was going to take, and of course Eeni wasn't going to run off on her friend if trouble reared its ugly feathered head. "I'll be fine out here," she told him. "You gonna be okay in there?"

"I'm just nervous," he admitted after a long, long pause. "What if my mother doesn't want to leave the zoo and come back to me?"

Eeni reached out her paw and patted Kit's tail, which was the only part of him she could reach. Having a heart-to-heart conversation with a friend's backside wasn't the best way to do it, but somehow not having to see each other's faces did make it easier to be honest. "It'll hurt if that happens," she told Kit. She felt her own hot tears welling in her eyes, thinking of her mother bound forever to the Rat King. "Life's more tangled and twisty than a tree root in a trash heap, but all the tangles don't mean the roots aren't strong. They just don't go the way you want all the time. But they grow anyway. No matter what, they keep growing. You get me?"

"I get you," Kit said.

"Anyway," Eeni added. "It's not gonna happen that way, because your mom will want out of this place right away. It's creepy!"

Kit snorted a laugh. "Thanks, Eeni," he said.

"You're welcome, Kit," she answered, and then the fur of Kit's tail slid through her claws as he crawled away into the building to find his mother, and Eeni was alone outside in the quiet of the night.

She sniffed at the sky and realized it was more like the early morning. The sun would start on its way up soon, and one way or another, the day would begin.

It was amazing to her how every day the sun rose, no matter what crazy things happened in the night. Night and day didn't know the worries of the folks who lived in them. They just flowed and flowed on past like a river, and every creature scurried along its current on claw and paw as best she could, never knowing which way time's river might toss her next.

And even as she got tossed about by time's rough waters, another creature would be floating by like a beaver on its back, carefree and unconcerned. Some night their places would switch and she'd be the one riding the smooth flow. The only thing folks stuck in time's river could be sure of was that the river would change. Happiness would change to sadness and then back again, but as long as you kept riding that river, no stretch of rough going would stay rough forever. It was a thought that comforted her, even as it made her nibble the tip of her tail with worry.

She'd been so lost in the deep water of her river thoughts

that she didn't hear the scrabbling of claws or the gnashing of teeth that crept up behind her until the massive shadow cast from the lamppost rose overhead. She whirled around to face it, claws up.

"Oh," she said. "It's you again."

Chapter Twenty

THERE IS NO
I IN *QUEEN*

THE Rat King had come to the zoo and towered over Eeni, silhouetted against the sinking moon behind them.

"You look worried, child." The Rat King spoke in a hundred voices from a hundred mouths. "Do you fear the failure of your plan or do you fear its success?"

"What?" Eeni replied, startled by the Rat King's sudden appearance, but also by the question. She lowered her claws and shook her head. "What are you doing here?"

"We are here to see you," said the Rat King. "But you

did not answer our question. Do you fear that your friend Kit may fail or do you fear that he may succeed?"

"Why would I be afraid of him succeeding?" Eeni rolled her eyes.

"Told you she'd be offended by the question," one rat voice in the tangle said.

"She doesn't look offended," said another.

"Maybe she has gas," said a third.

"I don't have gas," Eeni told them. "That was an offensive question."

"It is very rude to listen in on someone else's thoughts," the Rat King scolded her.

"Sorry," she said, "but I can't very well *not* listen when you're saying them out loud right in front of me."

"That is how we think," said the Rat King. "We cannot keep secrets from ourselves."

"Whatever," Eeni said. "Anyway, I'm not afraid of Kit succeeding. That's crazy. I'm a little busy right now, and I've already had enough riddles tonight and the baboons are a lot more fun than you are, so if you're just going to ask dumb questions, you can scurry on off with your mystic wisdom to some other rodent. I need it as much as I need my tail in a mousetrap."

"She's still angry at us," said one rat voice.

"But we came all this way," said another.

"She's not angry at us," said a third. *"She's angry at . . . me."*

There was a gasp, ninety-nine rats gasping as one and ninety-nine heads turning to look at one rat in the middle of the tangle. Ninety-nine voices spoke. "There is no *me*," they said. "We gave up *me* when we became *us*."

And then one rat spoke to the ninety-nine. *"She is our daughter,"* the rat said. *"She is* my *daughter and will always be. That is why we have come here."*

Eeni looked at the rat in the middle of the rats and knew her instantly. It had been more seasons than she could remember that her mother had been gone, but there she was, tail tangled with the rest, fur-matted like the rest, nearly identical to every other rat who was a part of the Rat King, but still, Eeni knew her.

"Mom," she whispered.

"Eeni," her mother whispered back.

"Well, this is getting weird," said another rat.

"Are we just letting this happen?" said a second.

"I'm not sure I like this," said a third, then covered his mouth with his paws. *"Eek! I just said* I! *Ack! I said it again! What am I doing?! Ah! Someone stop me! Ah! Me?! Eek!"*

A general mumbling broke out in the Rat King as all the rest began arguing among themselves, squeaking out loud all the thoughts a creature normally keeps to herself when she's having a bit of a panic. It was chaos and it was far too loud and Eeni had no interest in the Rat King's identity crisis. She wanted to talk to her mom.

"QUIET!" she yelled, then lowered her voice again. "We've got enemies at the zoo and you need to keep your voices down. Voice. Voices. Whatever."

"Apologies," said the Rat King. "There is no *I* in Rat King."

"I never understood that," said Eeni. "There *is* an *I* in Rat King. Right there in the word *king*. You really should've called yourself the Rat Queen. There is no *I* in *queen*."

"True," said the Rat King. "But the boy rats who started us would never have joined the Rat Queen."

"Well, that sounds like a boy-rat problem," said Eeni. "You probably shouldn't make it yours."

"Regardless," the Rat King said. "We are here now for you, whatever you call us."

"Yeah, well, thanks a lot," said Eeni. "But you're supposed to be wise, so you should probably show some wisdom and keep your voices down. We're in the middle of our escape."

"Which you are hoping succeeds?" the Rat King asked again.

"Yes!" Eeni threw her paws up in the air, exasperated and irritated and aggravated. Why would she *not* want Kit to succeed at rescuing his uncle and their neighbors and his mother? Kit had dreamed of seeing his mother again for as long as Eeni had known him. Of course she'd want him to save her and bring her home.

So what if that meant that everything would change. So what if that meant that Kit would have an uncle and a mother, while Eeni was still all on her own because her mother was a part of the Rat King? She'd been on her own before Kit came to Ankle Snap Alley. She'd be fine. She'd be *better* than fine. She didn't need a family of her own. And if Kit and his mother decided to leave, she'd *still* be fine because . . . because . . . well, she couldn't think of a reason, and suddenly she was crying.

The river of time had just turned into a waterfall on her.

What if Kit didn't need his friend anymore once he had his mother back? The Rat King was right. She really was afraid of him succeeding and as bad as that felt, she *also* felt bad about feeling that way. Scared and guilty about being scared.

And she didn't know what to do with all these feelings, so she looked up at the massive Rat King and asked, simply: "Can I talk to my mother again?"

"I'm here, Eeni," her mother said.

The wall of rats parted again to reveal her. She moved forward as far as her tangled tail would let her, so that she and Eeni could see each other nose to nose. They hadn't seen each other nose to nose since the night her mother left to join the Rat King.

"Mom, I—" she started, but her mother hushed her.

"*I know,*" her mother said. "*I know how hard this is for you. You're scared that Kit will leave you because you think I left you.*" Her mother reached out, took Eeni's paws in hers, and squeezed them gently.

"You did." Eeni sniffled. "You chose the Rat King over me. Just like Kit will choose his mother over me."

"*I wish I could help you understand that I joined the Rat King for you.*"

"Oh, thanks," Eeni jeered. "I forgot to be grateful that my mother abandoned me to become a hundred-mouthed fortune-teller."

"*The Rat King is not a fortune-teller,*" her mother corrected her. "*The Rat King is an idea. We are an idea that is so much bigger than any one rat. Before us, rats scurried by themselves through the world, fighting and scavenging and waging endless war upon one another. But every rat who pledges herself or himself to the Rat King is showing another way. When a rat tangles her tail with the others, she is pledging her fate to the fate of the others and her mind to the minds of the others. She is putting her life in the service of the group and showing us all that if a hundred tangled rats can live and thrive as one, then all ratkind can thrive untangled. We are showing everyone there is more to life than struggle and strife.*"

"So you didn't choose the Rat King over me," Eeni stated. "You chose all of ratkind over me."

Her mother frowned and looked like she might cry. Eeni knew she'd hurt her mother's feelings, but she'd spent a long time with her own feelings hurt, and it felt good to fling the pain back at her.

But it only felt good for the length of a breath. It hurt much worse after she'd done it. Hurt was not something that you could give away. The more of it you left behind, the more of it you had. Just like footprints.

"I'm sorry, Mom," Eeni finally said, trying to heal her mother's feelings and in the process, maybe her own. "I know you were just trying to make the world a better place for me. I know it can't have been easy to leave or to watch me grow up from afar."

A tear trickled down her mother's whiskers, but her frown turned into a smile and Eeni's heart lightened a little.

"And I know it must have been hard for you to feel you had lost me," her mother said to her. *"But I was always there, watching you with all the eyes of the Rat King, one hundred pairs of eyes watching your triumphs and cheering you on. There is room in the heart to love all creatures and to love one in particular. I am the Rat King and I am your mother. You are a hero of the Moonlight Brigade and my daughter. We are each more than one thing, and whatever we are is also what we were."*

"Yeah, yeah, yeah . . . life's a river," Eeni said. "I figured that out already."

"No, child, time is not a river," said the Rat King gently, a hundred soft voices, a hundred pairs of gentle eyes. "Life is not a river. Life is the boat upon the river, and you are not alone in it. No matter how rough the water or how storm-tossed, no one is alone on the boat, not you, not Kit, not even Titus the dog."

"So is that why you're here tonight?" Eeni asked, wiping her whiskers. "You came all this way just to tell me you're still my mom and to change my perfectly good metaphor about a river into one about a boat?"

"I'm here to tell you that whatever happens, it will be okay," her mother said.

"We all are here for that reason," the entire Rat King said.

"Seems like a lot of risk just to make me feel better," Eeni told them.

"The greater the task, the more the effort is worth," the Rat King said. "And what task could be greater than kindness?"

Eeni's nose twitched. It was hard to believe that the whole Rat King would come just to see her, but the thought made her smile in spite of herself. She didn't have just any mother. She had the whole Rat King who cared about her. She felt like a very important rat indeed.

"She's smiling," said one of the rats in the Rat King.

"Maybe she has gas this time?" said another.

"*No,*" said her mother. "*That's a real smile.*"

"It is," Eeni agreed. "Thanks, Mom. Thanks for coming here."

"A daughter's smile is worth the world," the Rat King said as one, and closed its rodent ranks around her mother, absorbing her back into the horde. "See you around, Eeni."

"See you," Eeni said, watching the Rat King scurry back to the shadows. She stayed in place, a smile raising her whiskers, grateful and proud, and certain that whatever came next for her and for Kit, she'd be okay. She knew she wasn't alone.

Chapter Twenty-One

THE NOSE KNOWS

INSIDE the zoo building, Kit had reached the Urban Wild exhibit quickly and slipped in through the air vent. The vent was so high that the animals couldn't climb back out through it, so Kit planned to open the lock from the inside and let all the animals walk out through the door on their own paws.

He dropped to what he expected to be the hard concrete ground of the fake Ankle Snap Alley, but it turned out to be soft. It wasn't concrete at all, but some kind of painted material that was gentler on the paws than the place was in real life.

He stood below the paintings of the buildings that were supposed to look real, beside the fake broken bicycle wheel, beneath the hard plastic tree, and he smelled the fake city air. The exhibit looked just like Ankle Snap Alley.

And the raccoon standing in front of him looked just like his mother.

But it was not the real Ankle Snap Alley in front him and he rubbed his eyes, for a moment fearing it was not really his mother in front of him either.

But she ran to him and hugged him and cried into the fur on the top of his head.

"Oh, Kit," she wept. "I thought you were as lost as the legs on a snake, but here you are! You're here!"

She squeezed him, her soft whiskers tickling his cheek, and suddenly the fake world inside the zoo felt more real than any place Kit had ever been in his life. He'd dreamed about this reunion for so long, imagined the things he would say to his mother, imagined the joy he would feel if he got even one tiny moment with her again, but now that it was happening, he found all words and thoughts and ideas were gone and he knew only one thing: he never wanted to let go of his mom.

But like sunsets and summer naps, all hugs must end, and even as Kit nestled his nose deeper into his mother's fur, he knew he had to pull away and get on with his plan to free her.

But not quite yet.

He squeezed her tighter and she squeezed him tighter and all the other animals in the Urban Wild exhibit would just have to wait. The whole wild world would have to wait for Kit to finish hugging his mother, because *also* like sunsets and summer naps, you can't stop a hug until it is ready to end.

He breathed in deep her musty-fur-and-flower smell and the scent brought him home to his burrow beneath the Big Sky, to all the memories of before, and it filled him with hope for all the memories he hadn't yet made. The smell made him sad and happy and hopeful at the same time. The smell made him feel safe.

Mother smells were powerful things.

"Oh, Mom," he said into her fur, which were not the most brilliant words a raccoon had ever spoken, but they were the only ones he could manage to think of at that moment.

When his mother let go of the hug, she held Kit's face in her paws and smiled at him. "Your uncle Rik told me all about the adventures you've had," she said, and the smile spread to her eyes.

"All of them?" Kit asked, peeking over her shoulder to where Uncle Rik stood, waiting.

"All of them," Uncle Rik said, stepping forward to give

Kit a hug of his own. "I told her you did a great job protecting me while she was gone, and I feel lucky to have had you come to stay with me in Ankle Snap Alley."

"Lucky?" Kit couldn't believe his fuzzy ears. Since he'd come to Ankle Snap Alley, there'd been brawls, and robberies, and fights, and kidnappings, and more missed meals than anyone could count. What about that could possibly be lucky?

"Some folks go their whole lives living in a cage," his mother said. "Safe as can be behind bars and glass. But life isn't supposed to be safe, it's supposed to be lived!"

"Birds are safe in the nest, but birds are born with wings. Better to risk flying, than to miss out on everything," Kit recited.

"You've been studying fox poetry!" his mother cheered. "Your father would have been delighted to know that. He was, himself, a lover of poetry."

Kit felt his whiskers sag and his heart with them. "Dad's really gone then? He's not also in a zoo somewhere?"

His mother stroked his cheek. "He's really gone," she said. "He fought to give us time to escape and he'd be proud of what you've done since escaping. I know he wouldn't regret a thing. A raccoon can't control when he comes and goes from this wild world, Kit, but he can control what he does with the wild time he's got in it and what he leaves behind after."

"From howl to snap," said Kit.

"From howl to snap," replied his mother, laughing. "You talk like a real Ankle Snapper now, huh?"

Kit nodded. "Oh! I have something of yours!" He reached into the pouch where he kept his seeds and nuts and he pulled out the wooden token with the symbol of the Moonlight Brigade on it. He extended it to his mother. She pushed his paw back toward him.

"It's yours now, Kit," she said. "You are the leader of the Moonlight Brigade. And from what I hear, you've got some mischief planned?" She grinned a wide raccoon grin.

"Kit's always got some mischief planned!" Dax the squirrel cheered from the branch of the fake tree, and leaped down in front of Kit. He raised both paws and smacked his fists together above his head, the squirrel salute. "Dax is ready for action, Kit!"

"I know you are." Kit smiled. "We're all busting out of here. All the animals in the zoo are. Well, *almost* all of them . . . Have you found the lock in here yet?"

"Of course!" Dax said. "Scoped it out the moment I arrived. But it's some weird box with buttons. Not like any lock I've ever seen."

"I know how to solve it," Kit said. He scampered over to the door in the wall and climbed up on the fake branch of the fake tree so he could access the panel that opened over the buttons. First, he tried the same symbols in the same order that had opened the baboon cage, but the answer to this lock was different.

Then he set his nose to work.

"Kit," his uncle Rik called up to him. "One normally picks a lock with one's paws, not one's nose."

"The nose knows a thing or two too," Kit replied, still sniffing the keys. There were four that held the smell of People fingers. Salsa and a hint of sour cream and hot peppers. Corn chips. And also, baby powder. Saliva. Paper and ink. Chocolate. The Person who had opened this lock last had had an interesting day.

He tried the one with the least powerful smells first. Mostly just baby powder and chocolate. Then he tried salsa, peppers, and sour cream, followed by saliva and chocolate, then baby powder, then ink and paper.

Nothing happened.

"Kit?" his uncle said.

"Just a moment," Kit called down. He tried another order, starting with paper and ink, then the chocolate, then salsa, then the one that smelled the most like sour cream, then the baby powder one.

That didn't work either.

"Kit?" Dax called.

"Hold on," Kit said. "Picking a lock with your nose is a lot harder than just picking your nose."

"Kit?" his mother called up.

He turned to look at his mother. She pointed to the wall of glass along the front of the exhibit and there was Preston, standing proud and smirking on the other side. Titus was beside him, standing on his back legs with his front paws against the glass.

Tap tap tap. Preston tapped the glass with his beak. "Hello, Kit."

Kit growled.

"Hey, Kit? Can you hear me?" Titus barked, his voice muffled by the thick window.

Kit braced himself. In his experience, whenever a Flealess got a smug look on his face like Titus had, something terrible was about to happen. He nodded that he could hear.

"Good!" Titus yipped. "I wanted to tell you that you and your family won't be going anywhere tonight!"

"And why not?" Kit shouted back. Titus cocked his head and pressed his ear to the window like he couldn't hear. "I said AND WHY NOT?" Kit repeated.

"Oh, because you'll all be eaten!" Titus laughed, and pointed up with his nose.

Kit followed his glance straight up to the air vent he himself had come through, just in time to see Basil the python, Atrox the rattlesnake, Naja the spitting cobra, and Thom the mad-eyed garter snake drop like falling branches into the exhibit cage.

"Breakfast is served!" Titus yelled, and cackled. "And lucky us, Preston," he added. "We get front-row seats to the show!" He banged the glass loudly, forcing all the trapped animals to cover their ears. "Let the games begin!"

"Thanksss for the nap," Basil hissed at Kit. "But now it'sss time for all of you to die!"

The python sprang at Kit, and the other three snakes charged forward, mouths open.

Chapter Twenty-Two

CAGE MATCH

ALTHOUGH the alley they were in was fake, the danger was very real. A dozen small animals trapped in a cage with four deadly snakes, and Kit didn't have a plan for this. He raised his claws, ready to fight for his life, but he felt himself suddenly yanked back, out of the way of the attack, and thrown behind the big truck tire. His mother had tossed him like a dandelion in a tornado, and at the same time stepped straight in front of Basil's open jaws.

Just as the snake smashed his jaws down, however, she danced to the side, rolled onto Basil's back, and wrapped her claws over his mouth, holding it shut tight. His tail whipped and slashed from side to side to throw her off his back, but she held on, calm and balanced.

Kit had forgotten: His mother was a master of claw-jitsu. He didn't have to fight on his own, not anymore, not with his mom by his side.

Basil thrashed, but could not shake the raccoon. He twisted wildly and his tail caught Uncle Rik across the snout, stunning him. Kit dragged his unconscious uncle to safety behind the tire so he wouldn't get caught up in the raging battle around him. Then he leaped back to the lock and started punching different-smelling buttons as fast as he could.

Salsa, sour cream, hot peppers, corn chips. Baby powder. Paper and ink, chocolate, salsa. Sour cream, chocolate, baby powder, ink and paper, corn chips. Smell after smell after smell, and still the door didn't open!

Atrox the rattlesnake had cornered the Liney sisters, three gray rats who went to school with Kit. Her tail was rattling and her nostrils flared. She rose up high over the rats, eyes like two eclipsed suns burning down on them.

But the sisters did not cower. They may have been young schoolrats, but they were part of the Moonlight Brigade, and Brigadiers did not cower! The little gray rats scattered in three directions, then attacked the rattlesnake from the three sides. They tugged her body back down to the dirt, grabbed her rattle, and stepped on her head before she could hiss out so much as a mean word at them.

"Never mess with sisters," the Liney sisters said together.

Meanwhile, Naja was a much greater threat. She'd gone after Dax and his mother, and though they had both raced quickly up onto the branch of the fake plastic tree, Naja launched a blast of venomous spit that hit Dax's mother halfway up the trunk.

"Ah!" she hollered as the toxic poison coated her fur. She fell, crying out and twitching on the ground. "I can't see! I can't see! I crrmm mmm . . . mrrrr . . ."

Blind and twitching, mumbling too, Dax's mother couldn't climb or even stand to fight back. The black-necked spitting cobra's poison caused temporary paralysis, which meant her victims lost control of their bodies before she ate them. While Dax's mother could no longer move or talk, she could still think and, even more terribly, *feel* whatever happened to her. For most small animals, the poison's effect would wear off after a while, but for most small animals, it wouldn't matter because by then Naja would have eaten them. The poison just made them extra tasty to the snake.

Dax leaped from his branch without thinking, and

took his mother's paw, trying to drag her to safety, but Naja was already there in front of them, another terrible loogie loaded in the little tubes of her front fangs.

Dax, desperate, did the unthinkable for a Squirrel of Action like himself. He used his brain. He observed the situation, looking at the whole scene, not just at what was right in front of his nose, and he thought up a plan. It was quick thinking, but it was still thinking. He was becoming a much smarter squirrel.

Instead of just diving into the path of the venom to protect his mother, which is what a Squirrel of Action would have done (and was just what the snake wanted him to do), he dove out of the way of the poison, letting it hit his mother again. She was already paralyzed, so one more dose wouldn't make much difference, and while Naja was spraying, her neck was extended and all her muscles were rigid. She couldn't turn on Dax.

It was terrible to see another spray of poison soak his mother, but it bought him the time he needed to flank the cobra, scoop up a handful of wood chips from the ground, and fling them into her eyes.

"Ahh!" Naja yelled. "I can't see!"

"Well, that makes you even with my ma!" Dax yelled back, then charged, delivering a high-flying kick to the side of Naja's head, following it with a chop to her cheek as she slammed into the ground. "Don't you dare mess with

Dax's family!" he yelled, raining kicks down on the side of her face.

He was so focused on pummeling her for what she'd done to his mother that he didn't notice her black body slicing through the air behind him like a whip. Her tail slashed across his back and sent him hurling off his feet. He landed with a *thwack* on top of his mother, and Naja rose again over them both, blinking the wood chips from her eyes.

"Now I will eat you both ssslowly," she said. "To be sssure your mother hearsss your ssscreamsss."

Across the cage, Thom the mad-eyed garter snake had cornered the gopher named Sebastian, who'd been an amateur magician back in the real Ankle Snap Alley. He'd pulled his head down into his neck and looked like he was trying to make himself disappear, but with no luck.

"Ha-ha-ha-ha-ha-ha-ha-ha!" Thom laughed.

Meanwhile, Basil had gotten the jump on Kit's mother, trapping her in his coiled body and squeezing her tight.

"Come down and play with usss, Kit," Basil said. "Or will the hero of Ankle Sssnap Alley sssimply let hisss mama sssufocate in my coilsss?"

Kit turned from the lock and jumped down in front of the python, ready to fight.

But he saw Dax and his mother about to be devoured and the Liney sisters gloating over their victory as Atrox readied for a counterattack against which they were not prepared. And he saw Thom about to make breakfast out of Sebastian.

Then he glanced at the exhibit window, and saw Preston the peacock looking away, disgusted by the violence he'd invited, while Titus was panting with glee.

Kit realized the little creatures of Ankle Snap Alley could not win this fight.

Maybe, he thought, if he surrendered, he could reason with the snakes. Maybe he could convince them to switch sides and join him. Or maybe he could at least trade his life for his mother's, like she had once done for him.

"Basil, stop!" he yelled. "I want to—"

But he didn't get the chance to surrender, because all of a sudden, there was a loud clanging above and all eyes looked up to the open vent one more time.

Baas and Chamcha's faces appeared in the opening, peering down at the scene.

"Looks like that mask-face got into some trouble," Baas said.

"A lot of froth and venom bubble," Chamcha said.

"Good thing we came back to launch a sneak attack," Baas added.

"Yes!" Kit called up to them. "Yes! Help us!"

"Mind your businesssss!" Basil hissed at the mongooses. "Thisss issss between them and ussss!"

Kit saw the python shudder, and the other snakes looked nervously at one another. Snakes had no fear of gophers or squirrels or even big raccoons, but in the wild where they lived, a mongoose could make a cobra cry mercy faster than a hummingbird drinks a drop of soda.

Then Baas said:

Kit is our business,

you forked-tongued goon.

From somewhere deep in the vents, the third mongoose dropped a beat:

Let his mother go,

or I'll eat you with a spoon.

"Not so fast! What is this?" Chamcha added:

We don't offer our resistance,

until Kit asks for mongoose-type assistance.

Kit stepped up, hope returning as fast as he could think of rhymes:

My friends of the fur, my pals of the paw,

your skills with a verse drop my jaw in awe.

But words aren't what are needed here!

My friends are gettin' bleeded here!

Snakes are gettin' feeded here!

Please!

I'm down on my knees!

Help me send these vipers slithering to the trees!

Kit dropped to his knees and held his paws open,

hoping his begging had worked as well as his rhyming, because if the mongooses wouldn't help, all was lost.

"Not bad, eh?" Chamcha said.

"Not bad," Baas agreed.

"Now wait a moment," Basil pleaded, unwrapping himself from Kit's mother and backing toward the glass wall. Then he started:

> No need to come down here . . .
> We sssurender . . .
> We'll go back to our cagesss . . .
> What . . . uh . . . what rhymesss with sssurender?

The other snakes pulled away too, retreating for the corners of the fake Ankle Snap Alley, but they had nowhere to go and the door was still locked and it was really hard to think of anything that rhymed with *surrender*. The snakes had been trapped by their cruelty as much as by their lack of wit.

Baas and Chamcha jumped down.

"No!" Titus yelled from the other side of the glass while the mongoose posse tackled his snake henchmen and, one by one, tied them to one another.

Outside the glass, Titus howled, and Preston hissed.

Kit turned to them and pointed. "You're next!" he yelled.

Preston and Titus looked from Kit to the knotted snakes and back to Kit. Then they ran from the building.

Kit had plenty of time to try his nose on the lock more calmly now, and after a few more sniffs and guesses, the door clicked open.

The animals of Ankle Snap Alley were free again, and so were Kit and his mother.

It was time to leave the zoo and go home.

Chapter Twenty-Three

THE AWFUL ALLIANCE

OUTSIDE, the sun was just starting to cast its morning shadows and Eeni still stood at her post by the vent.

She jumped when she saw Kit and the other animals round the corner looking exactly like they'd just fought off a nest of snakes. Dax had his mother slung across his back. She was snoring and moaning at the same time.

"Oh no," she said, rushing to Kit. "I was standing guard! I didn't see anyone come in this way. I'm so sorry. My mother showed up and I got distracted and—"

"It's okay," Kit told her. "They were ready for us before we ever got there. But we had some help and—wait! The Rat King? Here?" Kit looked around.

"Yeah," said Eeni. "But my mom spoke for herself. She wanted to let me know I had a mother too." She gave Kit a friendly punch on the shoulder. "See? You're not the only one who gets to see their mother again tonight." She smiled and Kit smiled back.

"This must be Eeni," Kit's mother said. She gave Eeni a hug. "Thank you for taking such good care of my son in Ankle Snap Alley. I hear he owes most of what he knows to you."

Eeni blushed a little. "I'm a helpful rat to have around," she said.

"Well, we'll have to make sure we keep you around then," Kit's mother said, and ruffled Eeni's fur.

It dawned on the little rat that she wasn't losing her friend so much as gaining her friend's mother. Her little boat was picking up passengers as it flowed down the river. She figured the Rat King's boat metaphor was a pretty good one after all.

"We better get going," Kit said. "The sun is up and the cages are opening!"

He looked around and saw that the baboons were doing their job with the Moonlight Brigade. The cow and the sheep were wandering the path, headed for the gate of the zoo, while Guster and Guster Two worked on making their hole below the fence bigger. The groundhogs they'd freed dug beside them.

"I didn't think we'd have to tunnel a cow out!" Guster shouted.

"Just dig faster!" Guster Two replied through a faceful of dirt, and they all dug faster.

Matteo the mouse was leading a pack of dingoes to freedom, while Hazel and Fergus had just set to work with Major Babi on the big gate to the Aviary, the big outdoor birdcage.

The birds sang a new song together: *"Shut your mouth and close your eyes, today's the day the free flock flies!"*

"Hey!" a Person shouted just as the birdcage swung open. "Blarg blarg blarg!"

"It's a zookeeper! Watch out!" Kit hollered, but Hazel and the baboons couldn't hear over the birdsong, and the zookeeper was running straight at them.

Kit charged into the path to stand in the Person's way, and the Person skidded to a stop, shocked at the raccoon in her way. Kit stood on his back paws and raised his front paws in the greeting of Azban.

"Blarh blarg blar blar?" the Person said.

"I greet you in the name of all animal folk," said Kit. "We mean you no harm but we are the Moonlight Brigade and we are duty-bound to free all the animals who long for the wild."

The Person's jaw dropped, nonplussed. Then she reached for something on her belt. Kit didn't know if it was a weapon or food or what it could be, but he didn't really have time to find out.

He dropped to all fours and snarled, then he charged at the Person, who let out a yelp of surprise, which sounds the same in any language. The Person stepped backward to get away from Kit, but Eeni had snuck up behind her, dragging a banana peel she'd found in the trash and she set it under the Person's foot. The zookeeper slipped and fell with a loud *oof* and Kit ran straight over her.

"AHHH!" The zookeeper covered her face with her hands, but Kit had no interest in biting or scratching her. He was very careful not to harm her in any way (except for the bruises she'd no doubt have from falling on her behind).

"Is this fun or what?" Major Babi shouted across the zoo at Kit, as he watched the birds take flight.

"Blarg!" the zookeeper on the ground shouted into the device she'd pulled from her belt. "Blarg blarg blarg," she said, and then looked up at Kit and said a few more things, which Kit didn't understand either, but he could tell were about him. Then the Person jumped to her feet and ran away into the bushes, still shouting nonsense Person sounds.

"I think the Person is calling for help," Kit said. "We better get going."

"No, you better not," said Preston, blocking the path in the other direction with his feathery tail plumed wide. "You've bested my snakes, but I knew a creature like you had many enemies. Titus suggested we contact them all."

Titus strutted up behind him, laughing. "I think you remember my friends."

Behind him, an army of Flealess marched in a row, animals Kit recognized from the homes around Ankle Snap Alley. There was Mr. Peebles the gerbil, and a large gray parrot, and two Siamese cats, and a big old bulldog with a bow in her hair.

"You're awfully far from home," Kit said. "Won't your People be worried about you?"

"Let them worry," Titus sneered. "It's time we got rid of you once and for all."

"And we found another old enemy of yours too," Preston said.

At his signal, from the other direction on the path, a large rough-looking creature stepped from the shadows into the morning light.

"Coyote," Kit gasped.

The big gray-and-brown coyote growled. "I don't much

care what happens to these leash lovers and cage cuddlers," he said. "But I cannot wait to tear you to pieces for chasing me away from Ankle Snap Alley. I had a long hungry winter, but I've a feeling this spring will be . . . *delicious.*" He licked his lips.

"How did you find all of them so fast?" Kit asked as the animals circled Kit and his friends, surrounding the whole group and pressing in on them from all sides.

"With some help from above," Preston said, looking up to the sky.

Kit followed the bird's stare and saw the broad-winged shadow of a hawk circling overhead.

"As you know, he sees everything from up there," Preston said. "And your enemies were quite eager for another chance to devour you."

The peacock let out one shrill whistle and then, in a flash, Valker the hawk tucked his wings and dove straight for them. He smashed into Eeni, pinning her to the ground beneath his talons with a shriek of "REVENGE!"

Chapter Twenty-Four

PRIDE

KIT rushed to help Eeni but was pushed back by the hawk's piercing golden stare.

"One more move an' aye'll crush her right now," Valker said.

"But we let you go!" Kit objected.

"Ay, but ya hurt ma pride," said Valker. "An' that I cannot abide."

"Nice rhyme," Eeni said, squirming in his grasp and trying to get back the breath the hawk had knocked out of her. "You should think about giving up this whole hunting-rats thing and become a poet. I'd be happy to write you a good review in the *Rodent Quarterly Journal*."

"Shhh, child. No clever words will get you out of this," Preston said. "Valker, you can eat the rat. You've certainly earned your breakfast."

The hawk fluffed his feathers with a happy squeal. He tightened his grip on Eeni as he prepared to smash her skull, but then he froze. His feathers tightened against his body. He looked at the bushes.

"What was *that*?" he asked.

"What?" Preston turned. "I didn't see anything."

"Aye've the eyes of a hawk an' you've the eyes of peacock," Valker said. "Trust me, Aye seen something."

"I smell something," Titus said, his dog nose working the air. "Something smells funny."

"I *am* known for my sense of humor," Eeni quipped from inside the hawk's clutches. She wasn't about to let her imminent death make her miss a good wisecrack.

"Not you, ratty . . . It's somethin' Aye don't—?" Valker didn't get the rest of his sentence past the tip of his beak before he was yanked off Eeni from behind and tossed tail feathers over feathery head into the bushes.

Jojo, the mountain of white fur and long yellow teeth, stepped over Eeni and lowered his head toward Preston, Titus, Coyote, and the Flealess. His heavy black claws clicked on the hard concrete path.

"You can all run away now," he whispered, so softly that he might have been singing a lullaby, but for what he said next. "Or none of you will ever run anywhere again."

"Eeep," Coyote squealed, piddling a little puddle where he stood. Then he ran away, sniffing frantically for the path that would lead him out of the zoo. Coyote was all snark and no fight and Kit hoped the he had finally learned his lesson and would never bother him or any of the folks of Ankle Snap Alley again.

The polar bear watched Coyote go, then watched Valker take flight, somewhat dizzily, in ever-widening circles until the hawk vanished in the clouds.

Jojo cocked his wide flat head at the Flealess house pets, who started to started to explain that they had no problem with him, but the bear licked his lips. They all went scurrying for their cozy houses on the other side of the city.

Only Titus and Preston Q Brightfeather remained. Titus barked and the peacock stretched his neck high, defiant.

"Jojo! You're out of your cage with People around! Isn't that dangerous for you? For bearkind?" Kit cried.

"I've been thinking about what you said, Kit, and some things are worth facing a little danger over. You need to be saved and I'm capable of saving you." Jojo lifted his nose and sniffed the air. "I would never be proud to call myself a bear again if I didn't help a creature in need."

"But you don't even know us," Kit told him. "You're risking your neck for total strangers."

"I was born on an ice floe at the top of the world where the sun never sets," said the bear. "I was shipped across the great salt seas to a city where the buildings cut the sky to slivers, and I was cared for and stared at and feared by creatures I could not understand and who could not understand me. I have seen more in my life than most folks will see in nine thousand lives. No one who walks this world is a stranger to me."

Kit stared at the bear, a beast the size of a mountain with claws that could flay the fur from his head in one swipe, and he stepped across the distance between them, stretched out his paws, and hugged the bear. He pressed their whiskers together and he held Jojo's head against his own. Kit was a scavenger and Jojo was a hunter, but for the count of three long breaths, they were simply two creatures grateful the world was big enough for the both of them. Kit let go and stepped back.

"The nerve of you, Jojo!" Preston complained. "I should never have imagined *you* would come to the assistance of these disgusting wild vermin. You are a proud and mighty bear, rarest in the world, and you have pride of place at this zoo. You live like the Lord of All Animals in here, but you know as well as I that you would not survive a day outside this fence. The zoo saved you from certain death in the far north! Why would you seek to repay its kindness by running away?"

"I am not escaping," he said. "This is my home. But a wise raccoon reminded me that"—he gave Kit a wink—"*we are All of One Paw*. So I will fight until the last snowflake falls on my face to make sure every creature who wants freedom can get it, and I will hope that the People will protect those of us who choose to stay. If you stand in the way of the Moonlight Brigade, you pompous painted pigeon, I'll be using your beak for a toothpick tonight."

The peacock looked from the polar bear to Kit and his mother, then back to the polar bear again. He looked past them at the baboons, who had found a food stand and discovered that hot dogs were more fun to throw than to eat, but that thick, sugary soda was the most wonderful thing they'd ever tasted *and* that it made them burp in fantastic fashion.

Two zookeepers were trying to calm the baboons, but they were outnumbered and the baboons were hopped up on sugar.

By the fence, another zookeeper was trying to herd the sheep away from the giant hole under the fence the groundhogs were still digging, while Camille and Clement, the ostriches, ran in rapid circles along the zoo's edge, chased by even more red-faced zookeepers.

It was chaos.

Preston shook his head at last and clucked at them all in disgust. "None of you are worth a single feather on my back," he said. "We had a good thing going, but it wasn't good enough for you, was it? Pfft. Go, then! Leave. I hope never to see any of you again."

And with that, he strutted away, trying to find a zookeeper he could walk beside until all the wild animals were gone.

"Hey, wait!" Titus called after him. "Where are you going? Preston! You coward! I came all this way to win! He's just a bear! Preston!"

But Preston did not come back and Titus turned to Jojo and growled. "Fine," he snarled. "I'll fight this bear off myself."

"You're brave, little dog," said Jojo. "I'll give you one more chance to run."

"Never!" said Titus, lowering his head and baring his teeth. Jojo reared back to knock Titus clear across the zoo, but then he stopped. He took a step back and flattened his ears. He lowered himself and looked for all the world like he was terrified of the little dog.

"That's right!" Titus barked. "Surrender and maybe I won't gnaw your nose off, you brute!"

"Jojo? What are you doing! Don't surrender!" Kit pleaded, but Jojo looked past Titus, and Kit followed his gaze to a zookeeper who stood on the path. She was the same one Kit and Eeni had tripped with a banana peel, except now she was raising a long strange stick to her shoulder and pointing it at the polar bear.

"That is called a *gun*," said Jojo, "and the People mean to shoot me dead with it."

Chapter Twenty-Five

THE WILDEST ONES

"NO!" Kit yelled.

"You have to run, Jojo!" Eeni cried.

"No," said Kit's mother. "He'll never outrun that thing. A gun spits metal sharper than a wasp's sting and faster than a hummingbird's heart."

The bear looked at the zookeeper, whose long gun shook in her hands.

"Look who chose the winning side?" Titus chuckled. "I wonder, if I start barking, do you think he'll shoot all of you or just the big dumb bear?" He grinned. "Let's find out!"

Titus barked and barked and with every bark, the zoo-keeper flinched some more. Jojo tried to look calm. He lay down flat, set his head on the ground, and tried to show the frightened Person he wasn't dangerous, but the Person still had the gun pointed at him.

"Stop barking!" Kit shouted, and stepped in front of Jojo to shield him from the Person and from Titus's cruel yapping. Then he yelled at the Person: "Jojo won't hurt you!"

"AHH!" the Person shouted, because she didn't understand Kit and Kit had frightened her by yelling.

In her fright, the Person fired the gun.

It made a loud *bang*, so loud that Titus jumped and tucked his tail between his legs, so loud that Kit's ears rang. He covered his eyes and waited for the stinging metal to cut through him . . . but it didn't.

He uncovered his eyes and looked up into an ocean of white.

Jojo had covered Kit with his body, shielding him. When Kit shimmied out from underneath, he saw the Person standing with the gun. Wide-eyed, Kit looked at Jojo. A spot of bright red bear blood was blossoming on his thick white fur.

"Jojo!" Kit yelled. "He's hurt!"

The other animals rushed forward to the bear's side. Even the baboons stopped rioting and the ostriches stopped running. Everyone paused to look back at the mighty bear. The zookeeper froze where she stood, gun barrel drooping, eyes darting around at the animals surrounding her.

"You saved me . . ." Kit grabbed Jojo's giant paw in his own. "You saved me even though you knew you might get hurt."

Jojo took a deep breath in and let it out. "All of One Paw," he repeated groggily. "Now go . . ."

"What about you?"

"They've subdued me now," Jojo said. "They're not afraid anymore. I'm sure they'll heal me. I am the pride of their zoo, after all." He raised his eyes and the other animals saw two more zookeepers had arrived. They had long poles with loops of wire on the end, but they also had bandages. "I'm sure they'll fix me up the moment you leave."

"But what if they hurt you more? What if they're still scared?" Kit's voice quivered with fear, watching the zookeepers' wary approach.

"I can't control how People feel about me," Jojo said. "They'll have to make that choice for themselves." Jojo looked again at the zookeepers, tried keep his ears flat, to look as meek as possible for such a big bear. "But I do hope they see I'm not their enemy."

"What about bear-kind? What if they retaliate against all bears?"

"Who knows?" Jojo said. "But if we need help—"

"The Moonlight Brigade will be there," Kit promised, standing taller. He gave the bear as big a hug as a raccoon could conjure. Jojo returned the hug as big as a raccoon could handle. Then Kit and his friends backed away. "You heard him!" Kit called out. "Go! Moonlight Brigade: fall out!"

Instantly, the baboons returned to rioting, swinging open the gate and letting out any creature in the zoo who wanted out. The ostriches made it first, leaving the rest of the Moonlight Brigade in the dust. The cow chewed on the grass in front of a building down the block, and all the birds took flight over the city. Some zookeepers went scrambling after them, unsure which way to run first.

"Stop the raccoon!" Titus barked at the zookeepers nearby. "He's the leader! Stop him first!"

But the nearest zookeepers were focused on tending to the bear's wound, and keeping him held down with their long poles. They didn't even notice Kit and his mother and Eeni and Uncle Rik slip off the path and head for the gate themselves. The last thing Kit saw was the zookeeper who'd been so frightened that she shot Jojo scoop Titus up in her arms and start to carry him away, looking at the tags on the collar around his neck.

"Hey!" Titus objected, his paws clawing at the air. "Hey! Where are you taking me? Let go! Let me go! Free me at once! I demand it!" the little dog yelled, but the Person didn't understand a word.

Once they reached the other side of the fence, the Ankle Snappers crouched in the grass and watched the People working on Jojo. The zookeepers didn't seem to be hurting him and he offered no resistance, but still, they looked frightened of the big bear. Two more zookeepers had arrived. Even as the other animals escaped, every one of them was focused on the bear.

Maybe Jojo would be fine. Maybe bearkind would be fine. Maybe not. Kit wasn't sure what would happen, but he'd never forget how the bear had saved his life, and he would make sure that the Moonlight Brigade was ready to defend bears wherever they found them, in honor of Jojo.

He just hoped the bears wouldn't try to eat them first.

"Let's go home, Kit," his mother said. "You did something amazing today, but now it's time to go."

Kit smiled. He'd done it. With some help from his friends, some baboons and mongooses, and a bear, he really had done something amazing.

Animals were free who'd never been free before. The wild world had just gotten a little wilder.

What would come next for them was anybody's guess. Not even the Rat King could know.

"I can't wait to tell the folks back in Ankle Snap Alley about *this*," Eeni said. "Blue Neck Ned will flip! He's gonna hate sharing his perch with all those big birds we just freed!"

"You can tell everyone tomorrow, Eeni," Kit's mother said as they padded away in a line along the side of the road. People out for jogs early in the morning jumped out of their way, then noticed the baboons racing along in the middle of the street and screamed.

"The sun's up and it's bedtime for both of you," Kit's mother told them. "I think it'd be best if we got back to Ankle Snap Alley and hid ourselves at home quickly. Who knows how People will respond to this breakout!"

"We'll be ready for 'em!" Kit cheered, but his mother gave him a look he hadn't seen in a long time. It was the look that all mothers of fur or feather, scale or skin, give their kids at one time or another. It was a look that no trickster could outsmart, and it spoke volumes.

"You'll be ready to go to bed," she corrected him. "Both of you."

Kit and Eeni locked eyes and they both realized they weren't orphans anymore, either of them. Their mothers were around, in one way or another. They had a bedtime. What other rules would there be? What else would change now that Kit's mother was back, and also now that the whole wild world knew Kit was ready for them?

He couldn't stop smiling.

Kit didn't know what would happen with the animals

from the zoo running around the city or with his life in Ankle Snap Alley changed completely, or with Titus still barking mad, but he did know that he'd have Eeni and Uncle Rik and his mother with him as they faced whatever the future held. They were a part of the wildest and most unpredictable thing in the world, after all: a family.

They would figure the rest out together.

C. Alexander London is the author of the middle-grade series The Accidental Adventures, Dog Tags, and Tides of War, and of the young-adult novels *Proxy* and *Guardian*. His most recent novels are *The Wild Ones* and *The Wild Ones: Moonlight Brigade*. A former journalist and children's librarian, he is now a full-time writer. He lives with his husband and dog in Philadelphia, Pennsylvania.

You can visit C. Alexander London at
www.calexanderlondon.com
or follow him on Twitter @ca_london

THE
WILD ONES

DATE DUE

JUN 0 6 2018	
	PRINTED IN U.S.A.